FIGHT! FIGHT!

"I'm ready for you," Slocum said.

Huggy swung a wide right, which Slocum blocked with his left. He drove a right into Huggy's gut. Huggy made a noise like a whuff, losing his air. He shot out a left, which grazed Slocum's temple. Slocum shook it off. He was inside the long arms of Huggy now, and he pounded Huggy's gut with both fists. Huggy was flailing at Slocum's back and sides with both his arms. Slocum suddenly straightened up, driving the top of his head into Huggy's chin. Huggy straightened then. He staggered back again.

"Goddamn you," he said.

Slocum had no mercy. Without warning, he drove a straight right into Huggy's nose. He knew he had broken it. It was squishy. Huggy staggered, then dropped to his knees. He was still holding his face. The blood was still running. He was making a noise that sounded like a combination of a growl and a whimper. Slocum looked at him for a moment. Then he turned and walked over to Speer.

"We never finished our supper," he said.

JAKE LOGAN

SLOCUM
AT HANGDOG

JOVE BOOKS, NEW YORK

THE BERKLEY PUBLISHING GROUP
Published by the Penguin Group
Penguin Group (USA) Inc.
375 Hudson Street, New York, New York 10014, USA
Penguin Group (Canada), 90 Eglinton Avenue East, Suite 700, Toronto, Ontario M4P 2Y3, Canada
(a division of Pearson Penguin Canada Inc.)
Penguin Books Ltd., 80 Strand, London WC2R 0RL, England
Penguin Group Ireland, 25 St. Stephen's Green, Dublin 2, Ireland (a division of Penguin Books Ltd.)
Penguin Group (Australia), 250 Camberwell Road, Camberwell, Victoria 3124, Australia
(a division of Pearson Australia Group Pty. Ltd.)
Penguin Books India Pvt. Ltd., 11 Community Centre, Panchsheel Park, New Delhi—110 017, India
Penguin Group (NZ), Cnr. Airborne and Rosedale Roads, Albany, Auckland 1310, New Zealand
(a division of Pearson New Zealand Ltd.)
Penguin Books (South Africa) (Pty.) Ltd., 24 Sturdee Avenue, Rosebank, Johannesburg 2196,
South Africa

Penguin Books Ltd., Registered Offices: 80 Strand, London WC2R 0RL, England

This is a work of fiction. Names, characters, places, and incidents either are the product of the author's imagination or are used fictitiously, and any resemblance to actual persons, living or dead, business establishments, events, or locales is entirely coincidental.

SLOCUM AT HANGDOG

A Jove Book / published by arrangement with the author

PRINTING HISTORY
Jove edition / December 2006

Copyright © 2006 by The Berkley Publishing Group.

ISBN: 0-515-14226-3

JOVE®
Jove Books are published by The Berkley Publishing Group,
a division of Penguin Group (USA) Inc.,
375 Hudson Street, New York, New York 10014.
JOVE is a registered trademark of Penguin Group (USA) Inc.
The "J" design is a trademark belonging to Penguin Group (USA) Inc.

PRINTED IN THE UNITED STATES OF AMERICA

10 9 8 7 6 5 4 3 2 1

1

Slocum had been sent for. As he rode into Hangdog, he reminded himself of that crucial fact. Looking at the sorry town, he could think of no other reason for riding into it. It had been a while since he had seen a more pitiful place. One road, one strip of buildings. It did not appear to be a place where anyone actually lived. It was a strip of businesses. Nothing more. As he moved on in, he could see that there was one hotel. It had a saloon on the first floor. Slocum thought that it must be a whorehouse, because he could not imagine that Hangdog would ever get enough visitors to support a real hotel. At the far end of the street, he could make out a livery stable. He saw a sheriff's office, a hardware store, a blacksmith's shop, a butcher's shop, a barbershop that advertised not only haircuts but also toothpulling, sewing up of cuts, and bullet extraction. Also a couple of small eating places and an undertaker's parlor. Wait a minute. There was another hardware store and another saloon. A nice place, this Hangdog, he thought. It don't look like anyone lives here but they got plenty of business.

He rode up in front of the hotel, if hotel it really was, and dismounted there at the hitch rail. As he was wrapping the reins around the pole, he heard a voice come from a man who was lounging lazily in a chair on the board sidewalk. The chair was leaned back against the front wall of the hotel, perched on its two back legs. The man in the chair was a hefty fellow with a mustache that might have been a handlebar if it had been waxed. Instead, it drooped, covering the man's entire mouth. The man appeared to be of an average size and was wearing black but dusty slacks, black worn boots, a dusty white shirt, a black slouch hat, and a black vest with a star pinned on one side.

Slocum looked up at the man. "Sorry," he said. "Did you say something to me?"

"I said, 'You're a stranger in town.'"

"How'd you guess?"

Ignoring the impudence of the remark, the man said, "I know everyone who lives around here. I can spot a stranger a mile away. Maybe farther. I been watching you ride in."

Slocum headed for the front door of the hotel. "Yeah," he said.

"What might you be doing here?" said the dusty man.

Slocum paused. He turned to look at the man, and he noticed the shotgun leaning against the wall just to the man's right. "I might be just passing through," he said.

"Are you?"

"I might be fixing to buy this hotel."

"I kind of doubt that. This hotel belongs to James Ritchie. So does half the town. I ain't heard that he's fixing to sell."

"Well, then, I might be just looking for a room for the night."

"That's more like it."

Slocum reached for the door handle.

"Why might you be wanting to spend the night in Hang-dog?" the other said.

Slocum heaved a sigh and moved over to lean on one of the poles that held up the overhanging roof overhead.

"You've got a heap of questions," he said. "I've had a long ride, and I ain't in a mood to answer them."

"My name's Thaddeus Speer," the man said. "I'm the sheriff of this town. It's a small town, and I guess I kind of mind everyone's business. We don't get many strangers in town. When we do, I'm interested. Well?"

"Well, what?"

"Well, are you going to tell me your business in Hangdog?"

"What if I don't? You going to arrest me?"

"Don't reckon I'd have a charge that would stick."

"I'm tired, Sheriff," said Slocum. "I'm going in to get a room."

He stepped back over to the door and jerked it open, but as he walked through, the sheriff was right behind him, and he heard the hammers on the shotgun click. He stopped still. The man behind the hotel desk looked up with wide eyes. The hotel lobby was a small part of the big room. The main part of the room was a saloon, and it was surprisingly busy for a place in such a small town with no houses in it. There was a stairway leading upstairs, presumably to rooms, but Slocum was too preoccupied with the shotgun behind him to take much notice of his surroundings.

"I'll just take your Colt," said Sheriff Speer.

"I won't argue with that gun you've got in my back," said Slocum, "but I wish you'd point it away from me and ease those hammers back down."

Speer reached forward and slipped the Colt out of the holster at Slocum's side. He tucked it in his belt with some difficulty because of his paunch. Then he eased the hammers down and lowered the shotgun. "We've got an ordinance against carrying sidearms in this town," he said.

"You could have told me that without poking a gun in my back."

"You're a stranger. For all I know, you might have

drawed it out and shot me dead. I'll have this in my office for you when you get ready to leave town."

"What about my Winchester?" Slocum asked.

"Where is it? Saddle boot?"

"That's right."

"Ain't no law against long guns," Speer said. "Have a good night—stranger."

Slocum walked on over to the desk, and Speer turned and walked out the door. The wide-eyed clerk stammered, "You—you looking for a room?"

"You have any?" said Slocum.

"Yes, sir."

"Sign me up."

The clerk pointed to the book, and Slocum signed his name. He paid for the room, for just one night, and got his key.

"Top of the stairs and to the right," the clerk said.

"Can I get a bath?"

"It'll take a while," said the clerk. "And it'll be another ten cents."

Slocum slapped a dime on the counter. "What's your name?" he asked.

"Ryan Walter," said the clerk. "I'll get right on the bath, sir."

"I'll be back," said Slocum, and he walked out the door. Unhitching his horse, he mounted up again and rode the length of the street to the livery stable. A skinny, scruffy little man met him at the door.

"Morgan Dyer," said the man. "What can I do for you?"

"Put up my horse," said Slocum. He read the prices on a sign posted on the front wall, and he dug out some coins and handed them to Dyer. "Feed him and rub him down. Put him in a stall for the night."

"Just one night?" said Dyer.

"So far," said Slocum. He pulled the Winchester out of the boot, untied and removed the blanket roll, and turned to walk back to the hotel. When he reached it, he walked to the bar and slapped the blanket roll and the Winchester on the counter in front of him. The bartender walked over, staring at the Winchester. "What'll you have, mister?"

"A bottle of good bourbon," said Slocum.

The barkeep poured the first drink, left the bottle, and Slocum paid him. "Tell me something," Slocum said. "Where do all these people come from?"

"Couple of big ranches outside of town," said the barkeep. "Mostly."

Slocum downed his drink, picked up his bottle, his roll, and his Winchester, and turned. He saw Sheriff Speer at the hotel counter. He smirked. He imagined that the lawman was checking his name in the register. Then he noticed that several of the customers in the saloon were wearing sidearms. He walked over to the hotel counter. "Hello, Sheriff," he said.

Speer turned to face him. "Howdy, Mr. Slocum," he said.

"I see you've done your snooping."

"It's my job."

"Well, you can drop the mister. I don't go by it."

"Just Slocum?" asked the sheriff.

"Just Slocum."

"I think I've heard of a Slocum."

"I ain't the only one in the country."

"No. I don't suppose you are."

"I noticed several fellows over there in the saloon carrying sidearms, Sheriff. You going to go over there and relieve them of that extra weight?"

"Nope."

"How come you took my gun and not theirs?"

"You're a stranger. And you wouldn't answer my questions."

"So the law's only for strangers?"

"Tight-lipped strangers, I'd say. I interpret the law as I

see fit. A man that just goes by the book ain't much of a thinker. I see you're toting your Winchester."

"Yeah. You said I could do that."

"Sure."

"Well, if you don't mind, I'm going up to my room now."

"Your bath's ready, Mr.—uh—Slocum," said Walter.

Slocum tugged on the brim of his hat, turned, and walked toward the stairs. As he mounted the stairs, Sheriff Speer, staring after him, said to Walter, "You find out anything about him?"

"Just the name, Sheriff," said Walter.

"He didn't say nothing about his business here?"

"No, sir."

"Um," said the sheriff. "Tight-lipped."

Slocum was settled into the bathtub with a cigar and a glass of bourbon. He had already scrubbed up and was just relaxing in the tub. In another few minutes the water would begin to get tepid, so he meant to enjoy it while he could. Then there came a knock on the door.

"Goddamn it," he muttered, and then in a louder voice, he shouted, "Come back later. I'm busy."

"The hell you are," answered the voice from out in the hall. "I'm coming in."

"The door's locked."

He heard him fiddle with the latch, and then the door opened, and David Mix stepped in with a wide grin on his face. "Busy, are you?" he said.

"Shut the door, you son of a bitch," said Slocum.

"I never expected to catch you like this," said Mix. "How the hell are you?"

"The question is, how are *you*? You sent for me."

"Yeah, I did, but we don't have to get right down to business just like that. We ought to get reacquainted a little bit first. What the hell you been doing these last few years?"

"Nothing to talk about," Slocum said, "and that ain't why you sent for me anyhow. What's it all about?"

"You ain't changed a bit," Mix said as he pulled a chair over close to the tub and twirled it around to mount it like a horse. He pulled a cigar out of his pocket and lit it with a match. The air of the small room was already filled with smoke from Slocum's cigar. Slocum grabbed the bottle off the small table there by the tub and handed it over to Mix.

"There's another glass over yonder," he said, nodding toward another small table that stood against the wall. Mix got up and fetched the glass. He went back to the chair and straddled it again and poured himself a drink. He took a satisfying sip.

"All right," Slocum said. "What's this all about?"

"Slocum, ole pard," said Mix, "since we parted company, I've had some pretty good luck. Been real fortunate. I struck some color out in Californee. Not enough to make me rich, but enough to get me started. Sold out my claim and came out here and invested in a cattle ranch. Did real good. Opened up a saloon and a hardware store here in town. Business is good too. At least it was for a while. Then Ritchie come to town."

"James Ritchie?" Slocum said.

"You've heard about him?"

"Just since I rode in. Your overly curious sheriff informed me that I'm staying in his hotel. Said he owns half the town."

"He was right about that. I own the other half."

"That well off, huh?"

"It's been a struggle since Ritchie hit town. He come in with a bunch of cash from God knows where, and he started buying things up. Took me by surprise. Just a little at first. Next thing I knew, he owned half the town, like the sheriff said, and not only that, but he's got a big cattle spread outside of town that rivals mine."

"That just sounds like business, Davey. How come you sent for me?"

"On account of I think it's more than just business. At first, I didn't. Oh, his hardware store took away some of my business, but really, there's enough to go around. I didn't let it worry me too much. Then he picked up some of my beef contracts. That hurt a little, but like you, I said that's just business. But lately, I've been losing some cattle."

"Rustling?"

"Looks like it. I can't prove nothing. Then I lost a freight wagon."

"Freight wagon?"

"Yeah. Well, I haul freight out of my hardware store. Ritchie does too. Anyhow, one of my drivers was scared off the road and dropped the whole damn thing, wagon and load and all, off the side of the road. That was a pretty serious loss. I begun to get suspicious."

"What do you mean about him being scared off the road?" Slocum asked. He put his cigar down in an ashtray on the small table and poured himself another drink. Mix downed his and reached for the bottle. Slocum handed it over.

"Well, Tom Caldwell, that's my driver, he said he was just going down the road when someone took a shot at him. He wasn't sure at first. He just kept on going, kind of looking around, you know. Then there was another shot and another. One of them hit the seat right beside him. That's when he lost it. He got kind of wild trying to get the hell out of there, and the wagon turned over. Tom was lucky to come out of it alive. He jumped just as the wagon started to flip. Got bunged up some, but he's all right. The worst of it was that he had to walk back into town several miles."

"What became of the shooter?" Slocum asked.

"That's the hell of it," said Mix. "He never showed. Tom

never seen him at all. There was the three shots, the wagon turned over, and that was it. Tom stayed down for a while, waiting and watching, but no one ever showed up. Finally, he tuck his chance and got up and started walking back."

"Did you recover the freight?"

"Some of it. Some of it was broke up."

"Was all of it accounted for?"

"Ever last bit."

Slocum picked up the stub of his cigar and had another puff. "Sounds to me like someone was just out to hurt your business. The shooter wasn't out to rob you. He left the freight alone. He wasn't out tc kill your driver. Just wrecked your wagon and went on about his business."

"That's the way I had it figured too," said Mix. "And that's why I suspicion Ritchie. No one else has got a damn thing to gain by hurting my business. Anytime my business is hurt, his just gets better. He done it, Slocum, but I just can't prove it."

"And that's the reason you sent for me?"

"That's it."

"Damn it, Davey, I ain't no detective."

"Well, damn it, Slocum, I ain't either, and I need some help here."

"What about your lawman, Speer, that his name?"

"Thaddeus Speer, yeah. He went out and looked over the wreck, and he even had a talk with Ritchie, but that's about all he could do."

"Yeah," Slocum sighed.

"I'll pay you well, Slocum. Hell, I ain't asking you to do this just for old times' sake."

"I know that, Davey, but—"

"But what?"

"Hell, let me get out of this tub and get dried off, get some clean clothes on, and we'll see what we can do."

"Good. I knew I could count on you."

"Don't count on nothing till it happens," Slocum said.

"By the way, your lawman took my Colt away from me. He said there's a town ordinance against toting a sidearm."

"There is," said Mix, "but the only time he uses it is on strangers. We'll get it back."

2

"Slocum works for me," Mix said, standing in front of the sheriff's desk.

Speer pulled open a desk drawer and drew out Slocum's Colt, laying it on the desk in front of him. He looked up at Slocum standing there. "You could've told me," he said, "and saved all this trouble."

"I didn't think it was any of your business," said Slocum, retrieving the six-gun and jabbing it down in his holster.

Mix slapped Slocum on the shoulder. "Come on," he said. "Let's go grab something to eat."

They walked out of the office and across the street to a small restaurant called Brenda's Place, and went inside. It was a little late in the day, and there weren't very many customers in the joint. Brenda was taking someone's money. Mix said howdy as they walked past her, taking a table against the wall. In another minute, she was there. Mix said, "Brenda, I've got an old friend here I want you to meet. His name is John Slocum. Slocum, this is Brenda James. She owns the place."

Slocum took off his hat and said, "Pleased to meet you, ma'am."

"Likewise, Mr. Slocum," she said, "but I'd be just as pleased if you'd drop the ma'am. Call me Brenda."

"I will," said Slocum, "if you'll drop the mister and just call me Slocum."

"It's a deal, Slocum. Now what'll you boys have?"

"Two orders of whatever is your house specialty today," said Mix. "Surprise us with it."

"You'll like it," she said. As she turned to walk away, Mix added, "And coffee, Brenda."

Slocum watched her as she walked. Brenda was a fine-looking woman. He guessed her to be around thirty years old. Her hair was reddish, not carrot-top red, but a nice light color, a combination of blond and red. He had noticed her blue eyes before she turned around, and a nice pair of full lips. Her bosom filled out the front of the shirt she wore underneath her apron, and when she turned to walk away, he could see that her round ass cheeks did the same to her jeans. Altogether, a hell of a good-looking woman.

"You like what you see?" said Mix with a grin on his face.

"She ain't bad," said Slocum. "Is she spoke for?"

"She's a widow woman," Mix said. "I don't know that anyone has spoke for her yet. Oh, there have been a couple that tried to move in on her, but she brushed them right off."

"What's wrong with you? I never knew you to be slow or bashful before this."

"It ain't that. I got me a woman, and she's got a mean jealous streak in her. I got to walk a fine line."

"You married?"

"No, but she holds a tight leash."

"I'd have never believed that about you if I hadn't heard it straight from your mouth," said Slocum.

Just then, Brenda returned with the coffee. She put it on the table and said, "Your food will be right out." She turned and headed back for the kitchen. Slocum watched her go.

"How long since she lost her husband?" he asked.

"It's been over a year," said Mix. "Long enough, I'd say."

"Um." Slocum picked up the cup and took a sip. The coffee was hot, hot and strong. As he put the cup down, the front door opened and Thaddeus Speer came walking in. As he walked, he yelled out, "Hey, Brenda, bring me out a cup of coffee, will you?" He stopped and looked over at Mix and Slocum, then walked straight over to the table where they were sitting. "Can you stand some company?" he asked.

Slocum thought about telling him no, but Mix prevented it by saying, "Sit down, Thad."

Speer pulled out a chair and sat. Brenda came out of the kitchen with a cup of coffee for him. "You want something to eat?" she asked.

"Just coffee," said Speer. She put it down and went back to her business. Speer took a long and loud slurp. "So, Slocum," he said, "how do you like our little town?"

"I guess I could take it or leave it," Slocum said. He didn't like Speer, and he certainly did not want to engage him in conversation.

"You got any leads on what happened to my wagon?" Mix asked.

"Nothing but three rifle shells," said Speer. "They could a been fired from any number of rifles around here. Hell, Slocum here carried a rifle that could have fired them."

Slocum gave Speer a hard look, but he kept his mouth shut.

"You find out anything from Ritchie?" Mix said.

"Nothing except that he seemed to be a bit tickled that you'd had some trouble. He said that he didn't have anything to do with it and didn't know nothing about it till I come in with my questions. But he added that it was bound to be good for his business. Said he was glad that Tom wasn't hurt none, and he said that the walk back into town probably didn't do him no harm."

"I figured he'd make light of it," said Mix, "but damn it, Thad, you know it's got to be him behind it. There ain't no one else who's got any reason."

Brenda came out of the kitchen with two big bowls of beef stew and a platter of corn bread and put it all on the table. "I'll get some more coffee," she said, and she was gone again. Again, Slocum watched her leave. Mix watched her as well, and then he gave Slocum a smirking look. Speer noticed.

"I'd forget about that if I was you," he said. "She ain't interested."

"What the hell are you talking about?" said Slocum.

Mix thought it best to steer the subject back to his problems as quickly as possible, so he said, "I just wish you'd keep a sharp eye on Ritchie."

"I always keep my eyes wide open," said Speer. "But you know I can't do nothing without proof. I ain't got hardly nothing to go on. Tom comes hobbling into town and says someone tuck some shots at him and run him off the road. I looked everything over and all I could find was them three shells. You can't expect too much out of that."

Slocum had taken about all of Speer he could stand. "I've learned over the years to never expect a damn thing out of the law," he said.

There was a moment of tense silence, and then Speer said, "I'm sorry to hear you say that, Slocum. I'm doing everything I can."

"Aw, he didn't mean nothing by that," said Mix.

Speer finished off his coffee in a gulp and got up to leave. On his way out, he tossed a coin on the counter. Mix said in a low voice, "There ain't no need to go riling up the law, Slocum."

"I don't like the son of a bitch."

They polished off their stew and another cup of coffee. Mix leaned across the table conspiratorially and said, "Listen, Slocum, I could go on out of here and leave you with a clear path. You just might get lucky with ol' Brenda."

"Bullshit," said Slocum. "Let's go have a drink. Then I'm going to hit the hay."

The door flew open, and Speer came bursting in. "Come a-running, Dave, your store's on fire."

Mix and Slocum both jumped up and hurried to the door. Speer was already gone again. The three men hurried to Mix's hardware store. The flames were already roaring and reaching up high into the sky. A bucket brigade had been organized, but they were mostly busy watering down the building next door to keep the flames from jumping over on it. Mix ran to the door, but the intense heat drove him back. People were running back and forth, yelling, gasping, shouting out orders to no one in particular. As Mix fell back into the street, Slocum stepped up beside him. "It's a loss," Mix said. "A total loss."

The firefighters fought mainly to keep the flames from spreading. No one believed that anything of the store could be saved. Slocum did notice that Sheriff Speer had obtained a water-soaked blanket from someplace and was beating at the flames. There was something to be said for the old fart. Slocum thought about joining in, but he decided that there were already so many, he would just get in the way. He stood beside Mix in the street watching the store and its inventory go up in smoke. He wondered how much of his money Mix had tied up in the place. He wondered how close to ruin this would bring him. It was bound to be a hard blow.

"Shit," said Mix. "Shit. Shit."

Slocum tried to think of something he could say, but words failed him. He wondered if Mix was right about this man Ritchie. If so, could Ritchie be responsible for the fire? Arson was a dastardly deed, and Slocum began having hard thoughts toward this man he had not even met—

this James Ritchie. It would take a real son of a bitch to pull something like this. He could feel the hatred boiling up from deep inside him. Davey Mix was an old friend. Slocum decided then and there that he would stay around Hangdog and do everything he could to find out for sure who was behind all of Mix's trouble. If it was Ritchie, Slocum would find the proof, and if the law would not do anything about it, then he would. He would not let Ritchie or anyone else get away with this.

When the flames had almost died down and nothing was left of the hardware store but a heap of smoldering ashes, and the nearby buildings were safe, Mix turned his back and started walking away. Slocum stared at the ruins for another moment, and then turned to catch up with Mix. As they approached the sidewalk on the other side of the street, a man in a business suit there spoke to Mix.

"Dave," he said, "tough luck."

Mix looked up, a snarl on his face. "It sure don't hurt you none, does it?" he said. He walked on. Slocum asked him, "Who was that?"

"James Ritchie," said Mix.

"Come on," said Slocum. "Let's get that drink."

They walked into the nearest saloon, the small one away from the hotel, and Slocum bought a bottle. He took the bottle and two glasses and led the way to a table at the back of the room where he could sit with his back to the wall. He poured two drinks and shoved one over in front of Mix. Slocum drank his down and Mix did too. Slocum poured the glasses full again.

"Davey," he said, "I just don't know what to say."

"Hell, Slocum, there ain't nothing to say. It's over and done."

"You, uh, you ain't ruined, are you?"

"No, I ain't ruined. I just ain't as rich as I was. That's all. I can still pay you, if that's what you're worried about."

"I wasn't thinking about that," said Slocum. "I thought you knew me better than that."

"I do, and I'm sorry I said that. I just . . . Well, I ain't thinking straight. That's all. I'm sorry, Slocum."

"Forget it."

Speer walked in, looked around, spotted them, and walked to their table. "It's a total loss, Dave," he said. "I'm sorry."

"Thanks, Thad," said Mix. "Wasn't nothing you or anyone else could do."

Speer glanced at Slocum and said, "Well, I'll be leaving you alone now."

"Hold on, Sheriff," said Slocum. "Sit down and let me buy you a drink."

Speer looked astonished, but he sat down. "What's the occasion?" he said.

"I saw you fighting that fire," said Slocum. "I was wrong about you." He waved an arm at the bartender and called for another glass. When it was delivered, he poured a drink for Speer. The sheriff drank it down, and Slocum poured him another. Speer looked at Mix.

"Dave," Speer said, "I know what you're thinking, but don't do nothing rash. First thing come daylight, I'm going to look the scene over real close. If there's anything to be learned over there, I'll find it. I'm going to question everyone in town too just in case anyone saw anything suspicious there before the fire started."

"All right, Thad," Mix said. His voice was dejected. He obviously was not expecting much.

"Sheriff," said Slocum, "would you mind some company in the morning while you're studying on the fire?"

"Why, no," said Speer. "Hell, no."

"I'll be there then," said Slocum.

Mix perked up a little. "Me too," he said.

They finished their drinks and got up to leave. Out on

the sidewalk, Speer said good night and headed for his office. Slocum and Mix stood there for a moment. "Where you headed, Davey?" Slocum said.

Mix shrugged. "Out to the ranch, I guess," he said. Just then a cowboy came walking up. Mix nodded at him.

"I'm sure sorry, Boss," the cowhand said.

"It's all over and done," said Mix. "Slocum, this is Charley Hill. He's the foreman out at my ranch. Meet Slocum, Charley."

Charley Hill and Slocum shook hands.

"Look, with what all's happened, and late as it is," Slocum said to Mix, "why don't you just go on over to my room and spend the night there? I'll give you the key." He dug into his pocket, but Mix just laughed at him.

"Hell," he said, "I've got a key. But I'll just take you up on that. Charley would you stop by the ranch house and tell Helen I'm staying over in town? I'll see her in the morning."

"Sure, Boss," said Hill. He turned and headed for his horse. Mix looked at Slocum.

"You coming along?"

"A little later," said Slocum. He handed the bottle to Mix and said, "Here. Take this with you."

Mix took the bottle and headed for the hotel. Slocum stood on the sidewalk thinking about all he had learned and about what had happened since his arrival in town. It sure did look like James Ritchie was the culprit all right. It looked bad for Ritchie. But Slocum wanted to know more. He began to understand the sheriff's predicament. You couldn't act just on suspicion. He pulled a cigar out of his pocket and started to strike a match, but he thought better of it and put them both back. He thought about another drink, but he decided he didn't really want it. He had about decided to join Mix and turn in for the night when he heard a small voice behind him call his name. He turned to look, and he saw Brenda standing there on the sidewalk. He tipped his hat.

"Hello, Brenda," he said. Then suddenly he realized that he and Mix had rushed out of her place not paying for their meals. "Oh," he said, "we never paid you." He dug into his pocket.

"That's all right," she said. "That's not why I spoke to you just now."

"No?"

"No. I just saw you standing here alone, and I thought I'd like to talk to you. I'm glad you're here. Dave has been having some real trouble. Tonight is just the latest and the worst of it. I've heard him talk about you. He thinks you can do anything."

"If he thinks that, then he's liable to be disappointed," Slocum said, "but I mean to help him all I can."

"I'm sure you'll be a big help."

"I hope so."

"So you two go way back together?"

"Quite a ways," Slocum said. "We were in the same out-fit during the war. Davey saved my bacon more than once."

"He tells it just the opposite. How far did you travel to get here?"

"Oh, just a few days. Not much."

"I'd say you're a real good friend."

"Like you said, me and Davey go back a ways."

"Yeah."

"Can I ask you a question, ma—uh, Brenda?"

She smiled at the near slip and said, "Sure."

"This James Ritchie. Davey's pretty sure that he's be-hind all his trouble."

"That wasn't a question."

"Well, do you know Ritchie?"

"Everyone knows everyone around here. Yes, I know him."

"Do you think Davey's right about that?"

She sighed and turned her back and paced a few steps away, then back again. "It makes sense," she said. "There's no one else who has anything to gain by Dave's trouble. But I—I just can't quite see James Ritchie in that light."

"You like the man?"

"He's always seemed to me to be a perfect gentleman. I can't help but like him."

"I see."

"Slocum?" she said.

"Yes?"

"You want to walk me to my place? I could really use some company tonight."

3

Slocum was not surprised when they walked back to Brenda's Place and she led the way around to the back door. Inside, he found himself in a neatly kept lady's apartment. So someone did live in Hangdog after all, but she lived in the back of her place of business. "Please sit down," she said. "Make yourself comfortable." She walked to a small bar back against the far wall and poured two drinks. She carried them over to where Slocum had eased himself down into the comfortable couch and handed him one of the drinks. Then she sat down next to him. He held up his glass and she touched it with hers. Then they both sipped their drinks.

"That's mighty good," Slocum said.

"I'm glad you like it. I don't drink much, but when I do, I like it to be the best."

"You've got a nice place here," he said. "It's a surprise to find it in Hangdog. I didn't think anyone actually lived here."

She laughed. "Running my own business," she said, "it's much handier than trying to keep a house outside of town. I don't have to worry about horses, about getting back and forth. It's much less expensive than maintaining

21

two places. Since—well, since I've been on my own, it just seems more sensible."

"It seems real sensible to me," said Slocum, "but then, you seem like a real sensible person."

"I try to be."

"Are you the only one who lives here? I mean in town."

"No. James Ritchie has a ranch, but he stays in town at his hotel. A few of his employees stay there as well. The manager of his hardware store has a place in the back of the store, much like what I have here, and he has a wife and children. So it's not really like I'm all alone here."

"Have you had any problems, being a woman all alone, a good-looking woman at that?"

"You mean with men?"

"Well, yeah. Some men are, well, you know. They can get pretty rough."

"I've been lucky, I guess. But Jim Ritchie and Dave Mix both kind of look after me. With those two around, I feel pretty safe. You know, between the two of them, they practically own the whole town."

"Yeah. I've gathered that. I know that Davey's got a woman out at his ranch."

"Helen Lester," said Brenda. "We're pretty good friends."

"What about Ritchie? Has he got any designs on you?"

She laughed again. Slocum thought that her laugh was a pleasant one. He enjoyed hearing it. "No," she said. "I think I'm like a little sister to him. He has a wife and family. We're all good friends too. James and Dave were both good friends with my late husband. We were all close. Since I lost my husband, they've all kept my interests at heart, I think. I don't know what I'd do without them. That's why I find it so hard to believe that Jim is responsible for everything that's been happening to Dave. I know what Dave thinks, but I just can't accept it."

Slocum downed his drink and thought hard for a moment. This was a real puzzle. He knew that he couldn't go off half-cocked against Ritchie, not without some kind of proof. It didn't make sense that anyone else was behind the troubles, though. There was no one who had a damn thing to gain by Davey's misfortunes. With the loss of the hardware store, Ritchie would have all of that business as well as all of the freight business. Davey still had some smaller businesses around town, and he still had his ranch, but he had been hurt by the fire. And Ritchie had gained by it. That much was for sure.

Over at the hotel, Davey Mix was on the bed and sipping from the bottle Slocum had given him. He noticed that there was part of another bottle in the room. That was good. He might drink it all before this night was over. He was frustrated, and he was angry. He was thinking about riding out to Ritchie's ranch and setting the barn on fire, turning loose all his horses, something to get even at least a little bit. Then he thought of just going straight for Ritchie and calling him out. In his drunkenness, he was sure that he could outdraw Ritchie. He realized that he was staying in Ritchie's hotel, and that thought burned him just a little, but then he realized that Ritchie had his apartment just downstairs. He could go down there and call him out right now. But Ritchie's family was there too. He would much rather catch Ritchie somewhere alone or in a crowd of men. He took another long swig from the bottle and lurched to his feet.

Crossing the room, he jerked open the door and lurched out into the hallway. Staggering to the head of the stairs, he stopped for a moment, weaving, then grabbed hold of the railing and stomped his way downstairs. He made his way through the lobby, weaving this way and that, and finally reached the front door safely. He knew where his horse was. He had decided that he was not spending the night in Ritchie's place. He was going home. He was going home to Helen. First thing in the morning, he would come back to town and join Speer and Slocum in examining the remains of the fire. Then he would tell Slocum to move out of the hotel and out to the ranch. He didn't like the thought of putting any money into Ritchie's coffers.

When Brenda had first approached Slocum out on the sidewalk, he had high hopes of getting into bed with her. Then he had walked her home, and they had started talking, and he found that his mind was changed. He was learning things from her, and he was consoling her. He suddenly found himself added to the ranks of those who would protect her, the ranks of Davey Mix and James Ritchie. She was genuinely worried about Davey and Ritchie, and before he knew what was happening, he found her head on his shoulder and his arms around her. He was consoling her, he thought. It was suddenly difficult to keep his hands still. He found them wanting to roam over her firm and sleek body. Why the hell had she come up to him on the sidewalk? Why had she asked him to walk her home and then invited him inside for a drink? Was it just to talk? He wasn't sure, and he damn sure didn't know what to do next. But then Brenda decided for him.

She lifted her head and looked up into his eyes. He stared into her lovely face for an instant, and then she raised her right hand, placed it behind his head, and pulled him to her, her lips meeting his in a kiss that was first tender, gentle, and then grew more desperate. She pulled his face to hers hard, and she crushed his lips with hers. In another moment, her lips parted, and her tongue plunged into his mouth, driving his lips apart, slurping, exploring, seeking around in his mouth, and he responded in kind. At last she broke away.

"I want to go to bed, Slocum," she said. "Will you be coming with me?"

"Wild horses couldn't keep me away," he said.

She stood and led him into another room, a room with a bed, nicely made up. She walked to the bed and pulled the covers down low. She turned and looked at him, and then she turned her back. Looking over her shoulder, she said, "Would you . . ."

Slocum moved to her and began unfastening the back of her dress. In another moment, she skipped out of it, letting it fall to the floor. She stepped out of the dress, leaving it in a heap, and Slocum began unfastening other things. Soon she stood naked before him. She put her arms around him and pulled him close. They kissed again. Slocum backed away and reached down to unfasten his gun belt. Hanging it on one of the bedposts, he sat down on the edge of the bed to pull off his boots, but Brenda quickly knelt in front of him to pull them off for him. He slipped his shirt off over his head and tossed it aside while Brenda fumbled with the fasteners on the front of his jeans. He stood up, and she slipped the jeans to the floor. Soon, she had him stripped, and she slid her hands up his thighs slowly, tickling as she went, until they reached his crotch, and then she gripped his sack and squeezed. His rod came quickly to attention, standing out long and hard and throbbing up and down. Brenda's right hand moved to grasp it, and she leaned forward to give it a quick lick. It bucked hard in her hand.

"Sit down," she said.

He sat on the edge of the bed, and Brenda inched forward on her knees until she was close in between his legs. She kissed the throbbing tool on its head, she licked it, and when Slocum thought that he could stand no more, she slurped the head into her mouth. Then she ran her tongue all around it. "Mmmm," she moaned. "Ohhh." Her left hand still gripped his balls, and she slid it under them and began a tickling motion with her fingers as she lurched forward with her head, sucking in the length of Slocum's rigid rod. She slurped back and forth a few more times, then stopped as suddenly as she had begun.

She crawled onto the bed around Slocum and stayed on her hands and knees, looking back at him with a teasing expression on her beautiful face. Slocum turned to look at her, her breasts dangling down, her legs slightly spread, her tight ass up in the air, and the damp, glistening muff tucked up neatly between the tops of her thighs. He did not wait long. He scrambled up onto the bed behind her and snuggled up against her, aiming his cock at the slimy slit she was displaying. She reached back with one hand to grasp it and to guide it into her waiting, moist hole. Slocum rammed forward, giving her the entire length all at once, and she gasped. "Ohh," she said. "Oh, yes. Pound me. Pound me hard."

Slocum drove as hard and fast as he could, his body slapping against her buttocks rhythmically. Slap. Slap. Slap. Looking around, he could see her dangling breasts shaking almost violently with the raucous movement. "Oh, oh, oh," she said. Not wanting to finish too quickly, he slowed his motions, shoving himself slowly and deeply into her, then drawing himself out slowly, coming to the very rim of her cavern, almost slipping out, only to inch back in again. After several such motions, he did slip out. "Oh?" she said.

Slocum fell down next to her on his back and reached for her. She smiled gleefully. "Oh." Quickly, she straddled him, mounting him like a horse, and she gripped the slithery cock, wet and sticky from her own juices, and held it straight up, positioning herself just right. Then she sat down on it, driving it back inside her, taking the whole length into her hot and waiting channel. "Ah," she said. She sat down hard on his upper thighs and lower belly. Their bodies were both wet with sweat, and there where the two came together, they were wet also with the juices that were flowing from her cunt.

When she moved, she slid easily back and forth on him. At first she rocked slowly, then more quickly, and then faster and faster. She cried out suddenly and stopped, throwing her head back, and then allowing it to drop forward again. She leaned forward, all the way down, resting her body on top of his, her breasts pressed almost flat against his chest, kissing him with a wet, wild kiss. "Oh, God, Slocum," she said. "That's once."

In a moment, she straightened up and started again. Over and over. When at last she said, "Twelve," Slocum grasped her hard by the waist and rolled them over. He was on top, between her legs, his swollen cock still deep inside her. He began hunching, driving, beating into her until he could feel the buildup deep inside. The pressure was intensifying, and he knew that he couldn't last much longer. He pounded again and again, and at last he gushed forth, a veritable stream flooding her insides. He stopped and lay still.

"That was wonderful, cowboy," she said.

David Mix had all but passed out in the saddle. He was maybe three miles from his ranch. His head wobbled on his shoulders, and his thoughts had stopped rambling. He was no longer thinking of killing James Ritchie, or of setting fire to his barn, or of turning loose his horses. He had stopped considering whether or not he should rustle Ritchie's cattle and drive them all across the border into Mexico. He was not even thinking about the loss of his store or of meeting with Speer and Slocum in the morning. He wasn't thinking about Slocum or Speer or Ritchie. He wasn't thinking of the lovely Helen Lester waiting for him at the ranch house, sleeping alone in the big bed. He wasn't thinking of anything. He was almost passed out.

He knew where he was going, but he wasn't doing much about it. Luckily, the horse under him knew too, and it was doing the navigating as well as the walking. "Oh, for a life on the rolling sea," he sort of sang as they plodded along toward home. His voice was not loud and strong, though. It did not carry a tune. It was a barely audible mumble. Mix knew nothing about life on the sea either. He had heard the song somewhere, and the one line was all he could remember.

He rounded a curve in the road, and a shot rang out in the still darkness. Mix felt something like a hard slap on his back. The horse lurched forward, and Mix rocked in the saddle. The horse ran. Mix bobbled. His hands grew numb, and he dropped the reins. The horse ran on. Mix fell forward against the horse's neck, and he bounced up and down against the neck as the horse ran on. Mix was out cold. The rapid motion of the frightened horse was too much for the inert body lying against its neck. Mix slipped a bit at a time until he was hanging down beside the wild creature. He was hanging on the right side. The only thing keeping him in the saddle were his boots in the stirrups, but the left boot was slipping with each of the racing horse's strides. At last it slipped free, and the body of Davey Mix slipped out of the saddle, but the right foot was caught in the stirrup, and as the horse ran on and on, it was dragging Mix along beside it. The wretched body, which showed no signs of life, bounced up and down on the hard road, and when the horse at last stopped there in front of the ranch house, panting and blowing, Mix, his right foot still hung in the stirrup, lay still there beside it, blood spreading on his back and chest, his face bruised and bloody, his shirt ripped and torn. He looked like someone who had been killed over and over, several times.

Slocum stayed the whole night at Brenda's Place. He got up with her in the morning. When they were both dressed, he went with her into the dining part of her building, and she fixed him a fine breakfast and a pot of coffee before she opened up for customers. Over her protestations, Slocum paid her for the breakfast as well as for the meal he and Mix had eaten the night before. The sun was coming up outside, and Slocum remembered that he had promised to meet Speer and Mix at the site of the fire. He left the restaurant and walked down the street. Getting close to the site of the fire, he could smell the ashes. Wisps of smoke still rose up from the heap here and there. He saw the sheriff walking toward him, and they met in front of the place where Mix's hardware store had been.

"A sorry sight," said Speer.

"Yeah. What do we do?"

"Just walk around, I guess. I ain't a expert on fires. I guess we'll just look to see if there's anything we can see."

They walked slowly across the front of the mess, Speer going one way, Slocum the other. Now and then, one of them would stop and poke at the ashes with a boot toe, then move on. They worked their way across the front and along the sides, and were heading toward one another again at the back of the site. "Slocum," Speer called.

Slocum looked up and hurried on over to where Speer was standing. The paunchy man was staring down at a blackened kerosene can. "By God," said Slocum.

"It was arson all right," said Speer. "It was done right here."

"Yeah," said Slocum. "I'd say you're right."

"Shit," said Speer, and he kicked the can as hard as he could, knocking it into the air and a few feet away. He stood staring at the ashes a moment. Then he said, "Where the hell is Dave Mix?"

"I don't know," Slocum said. "I thought he'd be here. He likely got pretty drunk last night. I'll go to my hotel room and roust him out."

"I'll be over to Brenda's Place having my breakfast," said Speer.

At the hotel Slocum found no sign of Mix. He went to the livery stable and discovered that Mix's horse was gone. He was thinking that maybe the crazy bastard had decided to go on out to his ranch last night in spite of everything, and he was going over to Brenda's Place to tell the sheriff, when Charley Hill came riding fast into town. Slocum stood waiting for him, and Hill reined up quickly right before him.

"What's going on?" said Slocum.

Speer was shoveling fried potatoes into his mouth when Slocum and Hill came walking in together. He looked up and nodded a greeting. They walked straight to his table.

"Davey's been shot," said Slocum.

"What?" said Speer.

"We found him in front of the house this morning," said Hill. "His horse had dragged him a ways. It took us a little before we could even see that he was shot."

"Killed?" said Speer.

"I thought so at first," said Hill, "but he's still alive. We patched him up as best we could. I figure he was shot out on the road, and his horse dragged him on into the ranch."

"You go on and finish up your breakfast, Sheriff," said Slocum. "I'm riding out to Davey's ranch."

"Never mind that," said Speer. "I'm going with you. Brenda!"

Brenda came out of the kitchen, and Speer paid her. Slocum told her what had happened, and the three men left the place together.

4

They found Dave Mix alive, but just barely. The bullet in his back had been removed by the old cook, Edgar Dunham. Mix had been undressed, washed, and bandaged. He looked like one of those Egyptian mummies that Slocum had read about once in some newspaper. Helen Lester let them in the bedroom for just a minute, and then ushered them out again. "He can't talk just yet," she said. "He did mutter a little when we first brought him in, but there wasn't anything he could tell us. I gather he was pretty drunk when he was shot."

"Well, thank you, ma'am," said Speer.

"Slocum," said Helen, holding out her hand, "Dave's told me so much about you. I'm sorry to have to meet you under such circumstances."

"Yeah. Me too," said Slocum. "I thought that he was staying in town last night. He went to my room in the hotel."

"He must have changed his mind. He's rather impulsive, you know."

"I guess so."

"Why don't you men sit down and have a cup of coffee?" Helen said. "Edgar will stay with Dave. I could use some company just now."

"Well," said Speer, "I really need to go out and check the road. See if I can find any evidence. But I guess it will keep a little longer."

"I got work to do, Miss Lester," said Charley Hill. "I'd best be getting to it."

"All right, Charley," she said.

Hill left the house and Slocum and Speer sat down at the table. In a moment, Helen had poured three cups of coffee and sat down at the table with them. "I knew something like this was going to happen," she said. "I told him to be careful. Charley had come by the house last night and said that Dave was going to spend the night in town. I was glad of that. Charley also told me about the store. Bad news comes all at once, I guess."

"I'd try to look at the good news, Miss—"

"Helen, please," she said.

"Helen," said Slocum. "I'd try to look at the good news."

"And what is that?"

"Well, Davey's alive. He could as easily have been killed by that shot."

"Yes," she said. "Of course. You're right about that."

"Miss Helen," said Speer. "I have to ask you—do you have any idea who might be behind all this trouble?"

"I have to agree with Dave," she said. "It's got to be James Ritchie. There just isn't anyone else, is there?"

"I can't think of anyone," said Speer, "but—"

"There just isn't," she said.

Speer and Slocum finished their coffee and took their leave. Outside the house, they stood by their horses for a moment.

"What do you think, Slocum?" Speer asked.

"I'm afraid that I'm in the embarrassing position to be agreeing with the law," Slocum said.

Speer gave Slocum an inquisitive look. "What?"

"There just ain't no evidence. Not right now. Not yet.

Ritchie bears watching, maybe questioning, but just because his business benefits don't mean that he's guilty. The evidence, if you can call it that, is all what you lawmen call circumstantial. Ain't that right?"

"Well, uh, yeah. You're right. It's real circumstantial."

"Let's ride on down the road a ways," said Slocum. They mounted up and made their way out to the road. Slocum noticed the drag marks right away. "These shouldn't be hard to follow," he said. They had continued down the road for a couple of miles, maybe more, when the drag marks disappeared. The two men stopped and studied the road. "Davey lost his saddle right here," Slocum said. "The horse started dragging him home."

"Then the shot had to come from right around here close," said the sheriff.

"Maybe," said Slocum. "He might have kept his saddle for a ways before he fell."

"How do we tell that?"

"I ain't sure. Let's ride along a bit farther."

They moved slowly on down the road another half mile or so, and then Slocum noticed, as they rounded a curve, that there might be a pretty damn good ambush site down the road. He stopped and dismounted. He moved into the brush along the side of the road. He checked out several locations before he found what he was looking for: a near-perfect lurking spot, well hidden, with a great view. He looked around on the ground and found a cartridge shell. "Hey, Speer," he called out. The sheriff came running.

"What you got?" he said.

Slocum pointed to the shell on the ground. Speer picked it up and studied it for a moment. "By God," he said. "This is where the shooter stood all right. This looks to be just like the others I found where the wagon was shot at."

"Look at this," said Slocum, pushing some brush aside to reveal a boot print.

"I'll be damned."

"Pretty small, wouldn't you say?"

"A little fellow."

"Maybe."

They looked around some more but found nothing else. They mounted up and rode into town. When they reached town, Speer headed for the hotel looking for Ritchie. Slocum went to Brenda's Place. There were no customers, and Brenda was seated at a table alone with a cup of coffee. She looked up anxiously as Slocum approached.

"He's alive," said Slocum. "That's about all I can say for him, though."

"Oh, no," said Brenda.

Slocum sat down. "Someone shot him in the back from ambush as he was riding home. If he'd have gotten attention right away, it might not have been so bad. But he didn't. His horse dragged him home. Beat him up pretty bad. Then he lay there in front of the house all the rest of the night before anyone saw him. He lost a lot of blood. His cook out there patched him up."

"Edgar's pretty good at that," said Brenda. "Oh. Let me get you a cup of coffee."

She was back in a minute putting a cup in front of Slocum and pouring it full, then refilling her own. She sat back down, leaving the pot there on the table.

"Davey's pretty tough," said Slocum. "I expect he'll recover all right. It'll just take a while."

"He'll get good care from Helen and Edgar," said Brenda.

"I think so."

"Slocum?"

"Yeah?"

"Will you stay around?"

"I wasn't sure till someone shot my ole pard," he said. "I can't leave now."

"Do you still suspect James Ritchie?"

"I never did. I mean, it might be him, but there's no evidence against the man."

"Are you hungry?" Brenda said. "Folks'll be coming in for lunch before long."

"Yeah," he said. "I could eat."

"Look, Sheriff," Ritchie was saying. "I know what it looks like. I know what people are thinking. There's no one to gain by Mix's problems but me. If I was over on the other side looking in, I'd suspect me too. At first I was glad to hear about his losses, because they were all in my favor. But now I sure do wish you'd catch the one who's been doing all this. Dave Mix has been shot and damn near killed. I didn't have anything to do with it. I swear it to you. I didn't have anything to do with it. You catch who did it, and that will clear me."

"Well, I hope so, Mr. Ritchie. I find it hard to believe that you'd be in on anything like what's been going on here. But I got to check, you know."

"Of course. Listen. If there's anything I can do—"

"I'll damn sure let you know."

The door to Ritchie's office opened and Cal Strother, the clerk in Ritchie's hardware, poked his nose in. "Oh, sorry, Boss," he said.

"That's all right," said Speer. "I was just fixing to leave."

Speer got up and Strother stepped in. "Come to think of it," Strother said, "you might be interested in this too."

"What is it?" said Speer.

"A big man come into the store. A total stranger far as I know."

"Go on," said Ritchie.

"He bought a whole mess of supplies. Like he was going on some kind of expedition or something. Spent a hundred dollars."

"Did he leave town?" said Speer.

"Drove out in a wagon," said Strother.

"Which direction?"

"Drove out headed west."

"What did he look like?" Speer asked.

"Well, like I said, he was a big man. Six-two or three. Weighed, I'd guess, two hundred forty pounds. He was wearing jeans and a red-and-black plaid shirt. Hobnail boots. One of those funny-looking little caps, you know, that snaps down in front. He didn't have no mustache or beard, but he sure did need a shave."

"Was he armed?"

"Not that I could see."

"Thanks, Strother," said Speer. "This might bear looking into."

Speer got his horse and started out of town going west. It wasn't difficult to find the wagon tracks. He followed them for quite a ways out of town. Then they turned off the road and headed across an expanse of prairie toward some low-lying hills beyond. There had been some mining there years before, but it had all played out. Could be, Speer thought, that some knucklehead still thinks he can find some color up there. Could be. He kept following the path of the wagon. It was nowhere in sight, and that meant that it must have gone into the hills. It was a hot day, and Speer wiped his forehead with his sleeve. I should have brought a canteen, he thought. He still had quite a ride ahead of him.

As he moved along, he rehearsed in his head what he would say to the man when he caught up with him. He had to try to find out the man's business. That much was certain. He was just trying to figure out his best approach. He couldn't just ride up and say, "Howdy, I'm the sheriff. What's your name and what's your business?" Or maybe he could. Why not? He plodded on. He sure did wish he had some water with him. He thought that his horse was thinking the same thing. He thought about the hills up ahead. He had ridden into them before, but it had been sometime back. There was nothing up there but a couple of abandoned mines and two or three old shacks that were about to fall in. It had been so long since he'd been up there that maybe they had fallen in by now. There wasn't much of a place for a man to go. And those hills just didn't seem to get any closer.

But he did reach them at last. He stopped and dismounted and mopped his brow. He looked up the winding trail that led up the hill. It showed signs of a wagon having recently gone up, but it looked like nothing else had used it for a while. Well, he was on the right track, but he wasn't at all sure just what he was on the track of. It might be just a scatterbrained miner. He mounted up again and started up the trail. The hillside was covered by a growth of scrawny trees and thick brush, and here and there it was trying to reclaim the road. In a couple of places, it must have been a tight squeeze for the wagon, but the tracks were still clear. It had gone up ahead of him.

Speer rode cautiously, looking from one side of the road to the other, looking always a bit ahead of himself. Suddenly, he felt as if someone was watching him. He could not explain the feeling. It just came over him. He stopped his horse and looked all around. He saw nothing but the scrawny trees and the brush. Something made him pull the Winchester rifle from the saddle boot, and he cranked a shell into the chamber. Holding the rifle ready, he urged his horse along slowly. Suddenly, there was a loud crack, and a bullet smacked into a tree trunk there just to his right. He dismounted quickly and ran for the cover of the thick brush on the side of the road. His horse nickered and turned and started back down the hillside road. Speer looked around, trying to locate the shooter. Another shot sounded, and the bullet hit not too far away. The man was either a bad shot or he did not have a good idea where Speer had squirreled himself away. But Speer had nothing to shoot at. He had seen no one.

It was suddenly quiet, too quiet. The shooting had stopped. Speer had to do something. He needed to get an idea where the shooter was so he could fire back. He was wondering just who the hell the man could be. He had been spotted buying supplies. That was no reason to go shooting at a lawman. There was something mighty fishy about this whole business. Speer made a quick decision. He stood up in a low crouch and ran across the road, and when he did the shots came again. This time there were four of them, and he could tell they came from two different rifles. Some of the lead kicked up dust just behind his heels. He crashed into the brush on the other side of the road and snugged down fast, thankful that he had not been hit.

But he had an idea now where at least one of the shooters was located, and he took careful aim. He fired, and he heard a yelp. He had hit one of them. But return fire came rapidly. Now there were at least three rifles, maybe four. He couldn't be sure. He could only be sure that he was damn well outnumbered. He wondered how far his horse had gone. He sure didn't need to be trapped out here on foot, but he couldn't fight three or four men, not when he couldn't even see them. He was afraid to go out into the road, so he started working his way down through the brush. It was rough going.

He made it down around a slight curve, and he thought that the road might be hidden from their view above, so he boldly moved out into the road and started down as fast as he could go. No shots were fired after him, so he figured he had gotten out of their sight. He ran faster, and he stumbled, rolling head over heels, turning several somersaults before he could stop himself. "Goddamn," he said as he stood up. He ran again, but a little more carefully. He could feel some scrapes and bruises on various parts of his body. He stopped and ducked into the brush again, looking back up the hill. There was nothing. He waited for a moment, then moved out onto the road again.

He trotted a little farther before stopping again. This time it was because he had to catch his breath. He was more than a little overweight, and he had not had a long run for years. He never went very far except on horseback. At the side of the road, he leaned on a skinny tree trunk and panted. At the same time, he looked up the road to make sure no one was following him. He seemed to be safe. His right hand happened to drop to his side against his holster. He slapped the holster and looked down. Damn. He had lost his Colt, probably when he took that tumble. He thought for a moment about going back up the hill to look for it, but quickly discarded that idea. He was worn out already from going down the hill. He did not think he could get very far going back up. And then there were those three or four men up there. Hell, he had another sidearm back in his office, and it would have to do.

He stepped back into the road and started down, but not so fast as before. He wasn't sure, but he thought that he was almost to the bottom. Then he could see the bottom of the hill, and he could see his horse grazing out on the prairie as if nothing was in the least out of the ordinary. "Knot-head," he said. He staggered the remaining steps down and onto the prairie. His feet were hurting him by this time, and so were the muscles in his legs. He was still panting from the exertion. And he began to feel the sting of the scrapes he had gotten tumbling down the hill. He stood for a moment staring at his horse. Then he started walking toward it.

He had a terrible feeling that if he were not careful enough about approaching the beast, he would spook it, and it would run away from him. He kept moving slowly and began talking low to the horse. "Don't you run away now," he said. "Just keep on eating that good grass. You don't get good grass like that in town, do you? You like that good grass? No. No. Don't move away from me like that. My feet are hurting me something fierce. You ought to walk on over this way. You would if you were a really good horse. No. Now I didn't mean that. You are a good horse. Yeah."

He was close enough. He reached out and stroked the horse's neck. He patted it, and he kept talking to it. He reached slowly with his other hand and took hold of the reins. Then he moved into position and mounted. "Goddamn," he said. "You knuckleheaded son of a bitch. Take me home." He kicked the horse in the sides and turned its head toward Hangdog.

5

When Sheriff Speer got back to town, he headed straight for the saloon in Ritchie's hotel. He found Slocum in there eating a sandwich and drinking a cup of coffee. As Speer walked by the bar, he called for whiskey and headed straight for Slocum's table, pulled out a chair, and collapsed in it. Slocum looked up at the wretched man. Slocum swallowed, and then he said, "What the hell happened to you?"

"When we split up a while ago," Speer said, "I went to question Ritchie, just like I said I would. Remember?"

"Sure. So?"

"So while I was talking to him, Cal Strother comes in. You know, his clerk over in the hardware store."

"I guess I do now. Go on."

"Strother says that some stranger came into the store and bought a whole shit-pot full of goods. Hundred dollars worth or so."

"Anything wrong with that?"

"Well, yeah. No. Not just in itself, but there ain't no reason for anyone to be buying up a mess of stuff like that around here."

Slocum recalled his own welcome to Hangdog and shrugged. "All right," he said. "Go on."

"Well, I went and followed the son of a bitch's tracks. Wasn't hard. He was driving a wagon. Followed him out of town and off the road. He went up into the hills where there's some old played-out mines."

"So he's a prospector who don't know they're all played out, or he knows something you don't know."

"I never seen no prospector outfitted like that. I got about halfway up the hill when they opened up on me."

"They?"

"At least three of them. My horse got off down the hill, and I had to lay and trade shots with them for a spell. I think I nicked one of them. Anyhow, first chance I got I scooted out of there. And I mean scooted. I took a tumble down the hill. Finally caught up with my horse and got back to town. Just now."

"If he was a prospector," said Slocum, "and if he knows something you don't know, something nobody else around here knows . . ."

"Like what?"

"Like them hills ain't played out. Like there's some real color up there."

"Not likely."

"If that's the case, then he could easy have partners. If there's at least three of them, like you said, they'd need more supplies than just one lone prospector."

"Yeah, well, how come they took shots at me?"

"They don't want anyone nosing around their digs. That's why."

"I don't buy it. They could be hired guns, hired by one side or the other to get this range war started up."

"That ain't hardly likely, Sheriff," said Slocum. "I know Davey Mix, and he wouldn't hire guns. Well, maybe he brought me on 'cause he thinks he sees that kind of trouble ahead, but if he was going to hire anyone else, he'd have let me know about it."

"There's Ritchie."

"He's so far ahead of the game right now, he'd just be throwing his money away. It don't make sense."

"I still believe they're up to no good, and I want you to ride up there with me first thing in the morning to check them out."

"All right," said Slocum. "I'll do it."

"How's Mix doing?"

"I ain't been back out there yet. I'd like to go out in the morning before we head up that hill."

"That's a good idea," said the sheriff.

Slocum had finished his sandwich and coffee, and he waved an arm at the barkeep for another glass. When the barkeep brought the glass, Slocum poured himself a drink from the sheriff's bottle.

"Goddamn it, they know we're up here now," said the big man who had done the shopping in Ritchie's store.

"Yeah, we have to move out."

"I'm hurt," said the third man.

"You ain't hurt that bad, Stopes," said Huggy, the big man.

"We got us a problem, though."

"What's that, Barber?"

"We got all them supplies in that wagon. We'd be easy as hell to track."

"Where the hell would we go anyhow?" Huggy said.

"I'm hurt too bad to be moving," Stopes said. "I need to lay still and rest up and get my strength back."

"There's a line shack over on the far side of Ritchie's ranch," Barber said. "I don't think it's being used. Trouble is, like I said, they'd track us right to it."

"If we had some extra horses," said Huggy, "we could pack all that stuff on their backs and ride over there."

"I tell you I ain't moving," said Stopes.

"Well, you can just stay here and fight off the law all by your own lonesome self," said Huggy. "Would you like that better?"

"Now cut it out," said Barber. "Ain't no sense in fussing amongst ourselves. Maybe we should just set it out here for a few more days at least. We didn't want no one knowing we was here, but what if they do find out? What then?"

"Ain't no law against us being up here," said Stopes. "Is they?"

"Not that I ever heared of," said Barber.

"We shot at that sheriff, didn't we?" said Huggy.

"Why, hell," said Barber. "We never knowed who it was, now did we? We was coming home with all them supplies, and we seen someone sneaking up on us. What was we to think?"

"That's right," said Stopes, a grin spreading across his ugly face. "We thought it was some bad man out to steal our goods."

"Maybe you're right," said Huggy. "But if we stay here, they'll for sure know where we're at."

"We'll say that we're mining for gold."

"Ain't no gold left up here."

"We just happen to think that there is," said Barber. "We're looking for it."

"Yeah," said Stopes. "That's what we'll say. And if anyone has a right to complain, by God, it's us on account of I'm the only one what got shot."

"You know them horses we was talking about stealing," said Barber, "so we could pack our goods out of here?"

"Yeah?"

"Let's get them anyhow. I know we can sell them across the border."

"Where we been selling the cows?"

"Same place."

"I can't go," said Stopes. "I'm hurt."

"Me and Huggy can get them all right," said Barber. "We'll go tonight."

The next morning Slocum and Speer were up early and had their breakfast at Brenda's Place. Speer thought that he caught significant looks between the two of them, but he decided to keep his mouth shut about that. They finished quickly and rode out to Mix's ranch, where Helen let them in. She was dressed in her riding clothes.

"How's Davey doing?" Slocum asked.

"A little better, I think," she said. "He's awake if you want to see him."

"Yeah," said Slocum. "We'd like to."

She led them into the bedroom, where Dave Mix was half-sitting up in bed propped against a bundle of pillows. He still looked awful, but he grinned a little when he saw them.

"Come to see what a dead man looks like?" he said.

"You don't look to be dead yet," said Speer.

"You only took one bullet, didn't you?" said Slocum.

"I had a hell of a ride home, though," Mix said.

"Anyone ever tell you you're supposed to ride in the saddle?" Slocum said.

"Oh, so that's my trouble. Well, hell, I'll know better next time."

"Dave," said Speer, "do you know who done this to you?"

"Ritchie," said Mix.

"Did you see him?"

"Hell, I was passed out in the saddle, but I know he done it."

"That ain't what I meant. What I meant was, did you see anything?"

"No. I never."

"That's what I was afraid of. I already had me a talk

with Ritchie, and he said he was real sorry to hear about what happened. Said he didn't have nothing to do with it."

"Course he said that."

"There's a gang of tough nuts hanging out over in the hills," Speer said. "I went out to check up on them, and they started in shooting at me. Me and Slocum are riding over there now to see what we can find out."

"Could be Ritchie hired them," said Mix.

"Could be."

"Why aren't they on his ranch then?" said Slocum.

"To throw you off the track maybe," said Mix. "Hell, I don't know."

When Slocum and Speer were leaving the house, Slocum again noticed Helen in her riding clothes. "You going out, are you?" he said.

"I ride every day," she said. "It relaxes me."

"I wouldn't go out too far," Slocum said, "the way things have been around here lately."

"I can take care of myself," she said. Just then Charley Hill came rushing up to the house. "What is it, Charley?" Helen said.

"We lost six horses last night," said Hill.

"Lost them?" said Speer.

"I think they was stole," said Hill. "They was in the corral. Now they ain't."

"Is there any way they could've got out by themselves?" Slocum asked.

"No, sir," said Hill. "They was let out or they was took out."

"Don't tell Dave," said Helen.

"Let's go have a look," Slocum said.

Hill led the way to the corral. The gate was closed. The fence was all in good shape. There were signs of other horses there, but they were not clear signs. There was no way of telling how many there were.

"It sure does look like someone came up and took them out," said Slocum. "Maybe we can follow their tracks."

He was wrong, though. After a short ways on the road, the tracks disappeared in a jumble of other tracks, wagon tracks, horse tracks going and coming. They had to give it up.

"Well," said Speer, "you ready to go on over to the hills?"

"Might as well," Slocum said.

They rode most of the way without saying much of anything. When they at last reached the hills, Speer stopped and pointed to a trail going up. "That's where they went," he said. "That's where I followed them, and we had that shoot-out."

"Well, let's follow them up there again," said Slocum.

They rode slowly, watching both sides of the road, but no one was there. Nothing happened. Close to the top, they spotted an old shack with a wagon in front of it. A small plume of smoke rose from the chimney. When they got a little closer, they heard an animal snort. "Back behind the house," Slocum said.

They rode on up to the house and dismounted. Speer stepped up to the door and pounded on it with his left fist. His right hand was on the butt of his revolver. They heard a voice from inside the house. "Who is it?"

"It's the law," Speer shouted. "Let me in."

"I'm hurt, but the door's unlocked. Let yourself in."

Slocum motioned the sheriff aside. He drew out his Colt, opened the door quickly, and stepped in and to one side. Speer came in after him. There was one man in the shack, and he was lying on a cot. His shoulder was bandaged. The bandage was bloody.

"I ain't armed," he said.

"Is anyone else here?" said Speer.

"I got two partners," said Stopes, "but they're out."

"Where'd they go?" Slocum asked.

"Out hunting," said Stopes.

"What happened to your shoulder?" said Speer.

"Someone come along yesterday and tried to rob us. We got into a gunfight with him, and I got the worst of it, but we did manage to run him off."

"That was me, you damn fool," said the sheriff. "How come you start shooting at me?"

"You? I'll be damned. We thought it was a bad man out to rob us. We had us a whole load of goods to protect. Damn. I'm sure as hell sorry that we tuck out shooting at you, Sheriff. We didn't know."

"Your partners out hunting for fresh meat?" Slocum asked.

"Well, not exactly."

"What are they hunting for?" said Speer.

"You ain't got to tell it around, do you?"

"Not likely."

"We're up here hunting for gold," Stopes said, his voice a near whisper.

"Hell," said Speer. "There ain't no gold up here. It's all played out. Has been for years."

"That ain't what we heared," Stopes said. "We heared that there's more up here than was ever tuck out. They just didn't look in the right places. We heared it from an old-timer what said that he'd be up here his own self except that he was all tuckered out."

"If you're really up here hunting for gold," Speer said, "when you leave, you'll be all tuckered out too, and you'll be broker than you was when you come up."

Slocum had been walking around the room casually, looking at whatever there was to see.

Stopes watched him nervously but didn't say anything. Finally, Slocum said, "There's been some trouble down on a couple of the ranches and some in town lately. You wouldn't know anything about that, would you?"

"No," said Stopes. "What kind of trouble?"

"A little rustling," said Slocum. "Small-time. Some arson. And a man got shot from ambush."

"Killed?"

"Not killed."

"I sure don't know nothing about none of that," said Stopes. "No, sirree. Don't know nothing about it."

As they were riding back to town, Slocum said to Speer, "I don't believe these men had anything to do with shooting Davey."

"What makes you say that?"

"Remember that little-bitty boot print?"

"Oh, yeah. Well, that fellow we talked to had big feet, and so did the one that was in the store. The third one might be a little fellow, though."

"Maybe," said Slocum, "but I doubt it."

"You don't believe them three is really prospectors, do you?"

"Not in a pig's eye," Slocum said. "They're up to some kind of no good. I just said I didn't think they shot Davey. That's all."

6

It was late at night when three riders came down on a small herd of cattle on the Ritchie ranch that was guarded by one lone cowhand. Ritchie had not had any cattle stolen, which was one of the reasons that Mix and Speer suspected him of being behind the misfortunes that had been plaguing Mix. No one was expecting any trouble. The lone cowhand did not see the riders coming. He was riding casually around the small herd and whistling an old tune. The cattle were grazing contentedly. All of a sudden, horses' hooves started pounding and someone shouted, "Get him." Shots were fired. The cowhand turned his horse to face the threat. He saw the riders coming at him, and he pulled out his rifle, cranking a shell into the chamber. He raised the rifle to his shoulder, but before he could pull the trigger more shots came from the three riders. Two of the shots hit their mark, and the cowhand tumbled from his saddle to strike the ground with a dull thud. His horse turned and trotted away. The cattle had started to panic. "Keep them going," someone shouted, and the riders moved after the cattle, still shooting and now yelling. They drove the herd south at a run.

• • •

Early the next morning, James Ritchie burst into Brenda's Place so abruptly that everyone in there sat up and looked. Ritchie stopped just inside the door and looked around till he spotted Speer seated with Slocum. He was followed on his heels by a cowboy. He hurried over to the sheriff. The cowhand followed. Speer swallowed hard and looked up.

"What the hell's wrong with you?" he said.

"Someone ran off some of my cattle last night," Ritchie said.

"And they killed Billy Boy," said the cowhand.

"Killed him?" said Speer.

"Jay here just rode in from the ranch to tell me," said Ritchie.

"Couple of riders rode out to relieve Billy Boy first thing this morning," said the one called Jay. "They come back to the bunkhouse in a hurry to tell me what they found. The cattle was drove off. Looked like a stampede. Billy was laying there shot—three or four times. Dead."

"This the first time you've lost any cattle?" Slocum asked.

"Yeah," said Ritchie.

"Who's he?" asked Jay.

"Oh," said Speer. "Jay, this here is Slocum. Slocum, Jay Everett, foreman out at the Ritchie ranch. Slocum's working for Mix, but he's been kind of riding along with me, helping out."

"Working for Mix, huh?" said Everett. "I ain't so sure that Mix wasn't behind that business last night."

"What makes you say that?" asked Slocum.

"He's been losing cattle, having other bad luck. He blamed Mr. Ritchie. Maybe he decided to get even."

"Yeah," said Slocum, "and maybe not."

"Maybe it's someone else altogether," said Speer.

"Like who?"

"Hell, Jay, if I knew that I'd have him in jail." He dabbed at his face with his napkin, then threw it over the unfinished breakfast plate and shoved back his chair. "I'd better get out there and look things over," he said.

Slocum pushed back his own chair. "I'll ride along with you," he said. He paused and looked at Ritchie and Everett. "If no one objects, that is."

"No," said Ritchie. "Go on ahead. But me and Jay are riding with you too."

Brenda had overheard some of the conversation. She stepped up to Ritchie and put a hand on his shoulder. He stopped and looked back at her. "Dave had nothing to do with this," she said.

Helen Lester was sitting beside Dave Mix's bed, her hand on his. She was leaning in toward him. "Is there anything more I can get for you?" she asked. There was an empty breakfast tray sitting on a table nearby.

"No," Mix said. "I had plenty. It was real good too. Thanks, Helen."

"I'll always be here to take care of you, Dave," she said.

"I ain't worth much right now," he said.

"You'll mend," she said. "Dave, there's something I want to talk about with you."

"Well, go on ahead," he said.

"Don't you think we ought to get married?"

"Well, sure. I figured we would before much longer. Then when all this trouble started, well, I guess I just kind of put it off."

"Let's get married right away. I'll send Charley Hill for the preacher."

"Right away when?"

"Now. Today."

"I ain't sure I can even stand up," he said.

"Don't worry about that," said Helen. "We'll take care of it."

"Don't you think it would be better to wait till I'm mended some?"

"I don't want to wait any longer, Dave. I want to be married to you now. I want to be Mrs. Mix. I want to be able to walk down the street in Hangdog with my head up high."

Slocum, Speer, Ritchie, and Everett rode out to Ritchie's range. Everett pointed ahead. "Right over there," he said. They rode on up slowly.

"Yeah," said Slocum. "I can see blood still on the ground."

"And looky yonder," said Everett. "You can see the cattle was spooked. They went out of here in a damn hurry."

"Let's see how far we can follow them," Slocum said, and the four men rode in the wake of the spooked herd. The tracks were clear. They had no trouble following. The herd moved south. They were still tracking near the end of the day when they drew near the border. Speer pulled up.

"I can't go over there," he said.

"By God, I can," said Ritchie.

"Me too," said Everett.

Slocum looked at Speer. "Go on back to Hangdog," he said. "I'll ride along with them."

Speer looked at Slocum for a moment. Then he pulled off his badge and shoved it into a pocket. "I reckon I can ride along too," he said.

They crossed the border still following the trail of the stolen cattle. There appeared to be three men driving the herd. Speer pulled up beside Slocum. "Three men," he said. "I reckon you know what I'm thinking."

"Our phony prospectors," Slocum said.

"That's what I'm thinking. The question is—are they working for someone or working on their own."

"I don't know how we'll find that out without catching at least one of them alive," Slocum said.

Up ahead at a small rancho, Huggy collected money for the stolen cattle from a scruffy-looking gringo. The cattle had

been driven into a small corral just beside the squatty little
jacal where the man apparently lived. Two other nasty-
looking white men lounged around a second corral a little
farther to the back. In this one were horses. Huggy and his
two partners grinned at the money they had made as
Huggy stuffed it in his pocket.

"Hey," said Stopes. "Some of that's ours."

"We'll split it up later," said Huggy. "Right now, let's
get going."

"Huggy's right," said Barber. "We don't want to waste
any time around here."

"Come back when you've got some more," the dirty
man said.

"You'll be seeing us," said Huggy as he mounted up. He
turned his horse quickly and rode away fast with Barber
and Stopes close behind him. They had not ridden far when
Huggy took a surprise turn.

"Where you going?" said Stopes.

"Take a different trail back," Huggy shouted. "In case
anyone follered us."

"Oh," said Stopes.

"Good idea," said Barber.

The sun was low in the sky by the time Slocum and the
others reached the little rancho. The dirty man who had
dealt with Huggy came walking toward them, his face
twisted into a sneering question. The other two lurked behind, leaning on the edge of an old wagon. Slocum reached
the man first. He hauled back on his reins and stopped just
in front of the man.

"You want something?" the man asked.

"We trailed some stolen cattle down here," said Slocum.

"I buy all the stock I have here," the man said.

"I'll bet you do," said Speer, who had ridden up beside
Slocum. Ritchie and Everett came up close behind. Everett
craned his neck, looking into the corral.

"There's our cattle right there," he said.

"You sure?" Speer asked.

"Hell," said Everett, "I can read the brand from here, and if I ain't mistaken, that looks like Dave Mix's horses back yonder."

"Let's take a closer look," said Speer. He nudged his horse forward, but one of the men leaning on the wagon suddenly cranked a shell into the chamber of his rifle and held it up ready to fire.

"Stay back," he said.

Speer hauled back on his reins. "Whoa. Hold up," he said. "Mister, all I want is to take a closer look at them horses."

"What for?" said the man standing in front of Slocum.

"I told you," Slocum said. "We're trailing stolen stock."

"And I told you I paid for all this stuff. If it was stole north of the border, that don't mean nothing down here."

"Mister," said Ritchie, "I don't take well to my cows being stolen from me."

"I don't blame you. If I was you, I'd take it up with them that stole them."

"What are their names?" Slocum asked.

"I'm a businessman name of Duffy. Maybe you heard of me? I got a reputation in the business. I don't tell tales. That's what brings me business."

"I never heard of you," said Ritchie.

"How'd a gringo like you get in business down here?" said Slocum.

"I bought this spread off a big ranchero," said Duffy. "I kind of keep him supplied with good beef and good horses."

Ritchie looked longingly at the cattle in the pen. Duffy was watching him. "I'll let you go over there if you want to kiss them good-bye, mister," Duffy said, "but that's all you're gonna get from here."

"Why you—"

"Shut up, Ritchie," said Slocum. "Boys, we've done all we can here. Let's ride out."

"We followed my cattle all the way down here, and I—"

"Come on," said Slocum. "Let's ride."

"He's being smart," said Duffy. "I'd listen to him was I you."

Ritchie whipped his horse around and started riding away. Everett and Speer followed. Slocum waited a beat, tipped his hat, and said, "Be seeing you, Duffy." Then he turned his horse and followed the others. They had ridden away from the little rancho far enough that they could not be seen when Slocum called out to them.

"Hold up a minute," he said.

They all stopped their horses. Ritchie gave Slocum a hard look. "What the hell is it now?" he asked.

"We didn't have much of a chance back there," Slocum said. "There was two of them behind a wagon with rifles ready. I say we change the odds around a bit."

"What you got in mind, Slocum?" said Speer.

"I got in mind going home with the cattle and the horses."

Slocum and the others left their horses back out of sight and approached the little jacal on foot. Each man was carrying a rifle. Each had his chamber loaded and was ready for a fight. When they got close to the jacal, they could not see any of the three men. Smoke was rising from the small chimney. They were all apparently inside, possibly preparing their evening meal. It was hot outside. There was no other reason for a fire. Slocum directed the men to spread out so that they had the house covered from three sides. They moved in more closely. Slocum raised his Winchester to his shoulder and took careful aim. He squeezed the trigger and easily knocked the flimsy metal chimney off the roof. The jacal was filling with smoke. Soon, it could be seen coming out under the door and out the windows. He could hear the men hacking and coughing inside. He saw a rifle being poked out a window. It fired, but the shot was wild. There was no way the man could have known what he was shooting at.

The front door flew open, and the three men came running out, rifles in their hands, firing as they ran. Slocum and the others fired back. Two of the men dropped in their tracks and did not move. The third made it behind the wagon. He fired a couple of wild shots. Four rifles barked, shooting back at the man, splintering the sides of the old wagon.

"Hold your fire," Slocum called out suddenly. There were a couple more shots, and then there was silence. There was a long silence. At last, the man behind the wagon, out of patience, stood up to look around for someone to shoot at. His rifle was up in his shoulder, but he could not find a target. A shot sounded from somewhere. Slocum did not know who fired it. He didn't really care. He saw the man stagger backward, twitch, and fall.

"Let's go get the stock," Slocum called out. "But move in careful. Someone in there might not be dead."

There was no need for the warning. Duffy and the other two men were dead as desert rocks. Everett went back for the horses, and in a short while, Slocum and the other three men were driving Ritchie's cattle and Mix's horses back across the border.

Back at Mix's ranch, Charley Hill brought Preacher Harp into the ranch house. Helen Lester greeted him with a big smile. "I'm so glad you could come out, Reverend," she said. "I know we didn't give you much warning."

"It's all in a day's work in the service of the Lord," Harp said. "Where is the groom?"

"He'll be out in a minute," Helen said.

The door to the bedroom opened and Dave Mix came out, held up by a cowboy on each arm. He walked gingerly, wincing in pain with each step. Harp looked as if he were hurting along with Mix.

"I ain't never seen a groom at the altar in this kind a shape before," he said.

"Dave had an accident recently," said Helen, "but we wanted to get married, and we saw no reason to put it off. I need to be with him now especially, to take care of him."

"That's a wonderful and godly attitude for you to take, sister," said Harp. "Now you fellows hold him up in front of that chair so that he can sit down soon as it's time. We don't want to keep him on his feet for too long."

"Thank you, Reverend," said Helen.

The cowboys moved Mix to just in front of an over-stuffed chair, and Helen moved to take her place beside him. Harp stepped just in front of them and opened his book to read.

"Dearly beloved," he said, his voice stentorian, "we are gethered up here to join this here man and woman up together in holy matrimony, which is a fine kind of a state to be in. Uh, kin you hold her hand, son?"

Mix pulled his arm loose from the one cowhand and took Helen's hand in his. He only wobbled a little bit.

Slocum and the others made it back across the border and relaxed a little bit. Speer pulled out his badge and pinned it back on.

"We gonna make it back in the dark?" he asked.

"I think we can make it without having to bed down," Ritchie said.

"One thing's for sure," said Slocum.

"What's that?" asked Speer.

"If those ole boys steal any more animals, they're going to have to look for another place to sell them."

7

The outlaw gang made it safely back to their shack in the hills outside of Hangdog. They rejoiced in the shack while Huggy counted their money and divided it up three ways. Huggy stuffed his share in his pockets. Barber held his out in front of his eyes staring at it. Stopes allowed his to drop to the table and scatter. Then he gathered it all up and let it scatter again.

"Boys," said Huggy, "let's go into town and have ourselves a steak dinner and then a few drinks."

"Is that smart?" said Stopes. "After what we just done?"

"That sheriff's liable to be after us," said Barber.

"Hell, he already knows where to find us, don't he?"

"Yeah," said Barber. "I was thinking about that too. Maybe we'd ought to move."

"Where'd we move to? Huh? Where?"

"Well, I—"

"I'm telling you, the sheriff ain't got a damn thing on us. Stopes told him we was up here prospecting, and that's all he knows. The only witness to what we done is dead. So what have we got to worry about? Nothing. Not a damn thing. I don't care if you boys come with me or not. I'm going to town."

"A steak would taste good," said Barber. He glanced at Stopes. "What do you say?"

Stopes thought a moment. He rubbed his wounded arm. "Let's go," he said.

Slocum, Speer, Ritchie, and Everett made it back to Ritchie's ranch, where they delivered the cattle. Then Slocum and Speer rode to Mix's place with the horses. Charley Hill met them there. He rode up quickly. "You got them," he called out. "Where'd you find them?"

"We found them across the border," said Slocum. He looked at Speer. "Me and Ritchie and Everett found them. Speer waited for us on this side. Your horses and Ritchie's cattle. I don't believe Ritchie's behind all this trouble you been having. Whoever stole these horses also stole his cattle. They sold them at the same place."

"You didn't catch the rustlers then?" said Hill.

"Nope."

"They got away," said Speer.

"What about the man who bought the critters? Would he tell who sold them?"

"Wouldn't say a word," said Speer. Then realizing that he had just given himself away, he added quickly, "That's what Slocum said."

"Any chance of making him talk?" Hill asked.

"Not anymore," said Slocum. "Him and his three pards are deader'n hell."

"You killed them?"

"They didn't want to give up the cattle and horses they'd just bought. I didn't see that we had much choice."

"I'll be damned," said Hill. "So it ain't Ritchie."

"I'd place a bet on it," said Slocum. "How's Davey doing?"

"He's coming along. Stood up and got hitched yesterday."

"He did?" said Slocum. "Well, I'll be damned. You reckon we can bust in on him and see how he's doing?"

"I don't see no reason against it. I can take care of these horses now if you want to ride on over to the house."

"Thanks," said Slocum. "We'll do that."

Helen opened the door after Slocum knocked. "Oh," she said, surprised. "Hello, Slocum, Sheriff. Won't you come in?"

Slocum and Speer removed their hats and stepped inside.

"I guess it's Mrs. Mix now," said Slocum.

She smiled. "That's right," she said. "I suppose you came to see Dave? I believe he's awake and sitting up. Follow me."

She crossed the room and stood in the bedroom doorway. "Dave, you have visitors," she said. Then she stepped out of the way to allow the two men to enter.

"Slocum," said Mix, a broad grin spreading across his face. "Thaddeus. Come on in. What the hell have you two been up to?"

"We've got some news for you, Davey," Slocum said.

"Is it good news?"

"Well, I think it is."

"Let me have it then."

"I kind of wanted to ask you how you're feeling first," Slocum said.

"Aw, I'm doing all right. I'll be up and out of this bed in another day or two. What's the news?"

"We heard there was a wedding here," said Speer.

"Oh, yeah," said Mix. "Me and Helen got ourselves hitched up."

"That was kind of sudden, wasn't it?" said Slocum.

"Naw. We'd been planning it all along. We just decided to go on ahead and do it. That's all. Now what's the news?"

Slocum wrinkled his brow at Mix's response, but he didn't say anything about it. Instead, he said, "You had some horses stole. Did anyone tell you about it?"

"No," said Mix, sitting up straighter, an angry look spreading over his face. "Why the hell—"

"Hold on," Slocum said. "We thought it best not to worry you with it. Not till we got them back."

"Did you?"

"We just brought them in."

"Who done it? Ritchie?"

"Whoever done it stole some of Ritchie's cattle at about the same time," Slocum said. "We found them all together down across the border. They'd all been sold to the same buyer. He wouldn't talk, and he wouldn't give up the animals either. Not till we killed him and his pards."

"So you still don't know who's responsible?"

"No," Slocum said. "But it's pretty damn sure that it ain't Ritchie."

"Goddamn," said Mix. "I really thought it was him. I sure did."

"I told you all along you was jumping the gun," said Speer.

"Yeah," said Mix. "I guess you did. I guess I might just owe Ritchie an apology."

"You want us to send him out to see you?" Speer asked.

"Yeah," said Mix. "Not just now, though. Give me a couple of days. Tell him I ain't quite up to it just now. Okay?"

"Okay," Speer said.

"Not Ritchie," said Mix. "I wonder who the hell it is."

"We've got a pretty good idea," said the sheriff. "We just ain't got proof. At least not yet. We're watching them, though."

"Well?" said Mix. "Who is it?"

"Three scruffy-looking bastards staying at one of them abandoned shacks up on the hill with the old abandoned mines. Claim they're prospecting."

"That don't make sense," said Mix.

"That's what I told them. They said they know something I don't know. They could just be three fools chasing after a rainbow. But I'm suspicious."

"Keep me informed, will you?" said Mix.

"You bet."

Huggy and his partners rode into Hangdog and tied their horses in front of Brenda's Place. There was a small crowd already eating. They found one of the few tables left and sat down. Most of Brenda's customers looked at them with curiosity. Not that many strangers came through Hangdog, and these three were especially curious. Ragged and dirty, they had the look of wolfers, or just tramps. They did not look like the kind of people to come into a respectable restaurant and order a meal. Brenda came over to their table. "What can I do for you?" she asked.

"We come in to eat," Stopes said.

"Well, that's what I'm here for," Brenda said.

"Steaks," said Huggy. "Three big juicy steaks."

"Taters and bread and gravy and beans," said Barber.

"You want three steaks with potatoes, gravy, and beans on the side? Is that right?"

"And bread," said Barber.

"Bread comes with it," said Brenda. "Something to drink?"

"You got whiskey?"

"No. I'm sorry. I'm not allowed to sell whiskey in here. You'll have to go over to one of the saloons for that."

"Bring us some coffee," said Huggy. "That'll do."

Outside, Slocum and Speer were riding into town. "You hungry, Speer?" Slocum asked.

"We ain't et all day," said Speer. "Course I'm hungry."

"Brenda's?"

"Sure."

They dismounted and tied their horses in front of Brenda's Place. "Looks busy," said Speer.

"Maybe she'll get rich," said Slocum.

"By God," said Speer, "I hope she does."

They stepped inside and immediately, they both spotted the phony prospectors. Speer started to make a move, but Slocum stopped him. "Let's just eat," he said. They sat down and ordered their meal. Soon, they were drinking coffee. Both of them were watching the three men. They watched when Brenda delivered their steaks and refilled their cups, and they watched when the three men dug into their food like they had never eaten out in public before. Grease ran down Huggy's chin, and he wiped it off with his grimy sleeve. In another minute, Slocum's and Speer's meals were served to them. They ate, but they kept watching the three men. Huggy noticed Speer's badge.

"Don't twist your necks, boys," he said in a low voice, "but the sheriff's over yonder looking at us."

"I told you—"

"Shut up, Stopes," said Huggy. "There ain't a damn thing he can do."

"Don't let it spoil your eats," said Barber. "He ain't even spoke to us. He's just in here eating, same as us."

"He's sure looking, though," said Stopes.

They finished their meal in silence, and Huggy said, "Let's get out of here." They stood up and walked toward the door, pausing at the counter to pay. Then they went outside. Slocum and Speer looked at each other.

"You had enough?" Slocum asked.

"I'm plumb full," said Speer.

They stood up, leaving half their meals on their plates, tossed some money on the counter, and walked outside just in time to see the three men duck into Ritchie's hotel.

"They're going for a drink," said Speer.

"I doubt if they're looking for rooms," said Slocum.

They followed the three men. Inside the hotel, they turned into the saloon. The three men were sitting at a table near the bar. Slocum got two glasses from the barkeep. He looked at Speer and said, "Let's have a talk with them."

"All right," said Speer.

They walked to the table where the three were sitting, pulled out chairs, and sat down.

"You don't mind, do you?" said Speer.

"Why, hell, no," said Huggy. He figured the sheriff was Speer.

Slocum grabbed their bottle and poured himself and Speer a drink. "You did say you'd buy us a drink, didn't you?" he asked.

"Now, wait a minute—"

Stopes had started to say something, but Huggy kicked him under the table. "Sure," Huggy said. "It's on us."

Slocum turned up his glass and emptied it. He reached for the bottle again. "This ain't bad whiskey," he said. "It ain't the best, but it ain't bad."

"Well, uh, what you fellows been up to?" Huggy asked.

"Chasing stolen cows and horses," Slocum said.

"Oh?"

"We got them all right," said Speer. "Took them back to their owners."

"Did you, uh, get the men what stole them?" said Huggy.

"No," said Speer, "but we got them men that bought them."

"Oh, yeah? Where at?"

"Across the border," Slocum said. "We had to kill them."

"All three of them," said Speer.

"Dead as rocks," said Slocum.

"Killed them dead, huh?" said Stopes. He was sweating. Barber was fidgeting with his glass. Huggy drank his glass empty and poured himself a refill.

"So," he said, "you got no idea who done the actual thieving?"

"I never said we had no idea," Speer said. "I have a pretty good idea."

"You boys seem to have plenty of spending money," said Slocum. "You dig up some gold, did you?"

"Yeah," blurted Stopes.

"No," said Barber.

"Well, which is it?" said Speer.

"It ain't neither one," said Huggy. "I mean, it ain't none of your damn business. We just got some money is all, and we don't have to tell you where we got it. Is there any law what says we got to tell you where we got our money? Well, is there?"

"No law," said Speer. "I just thought you might want to be cooperating with the sheriff's office. That's all. I thought maybe you were good citizens."

"We are," said Stopes. He looked at Barber. "Ain't we?"

"Yeah. We are."

Slocum, Speer, Stopes, and Barber all looked at Huggy. He hesitated a moment. Then he smiled, showing his discolored teeth.

"Yeah, well," he said, "since you put it that way, I'll tell you where we got it. We got it from a good friend. He give us a stake whenever we tell him we's going prospecting. When we strike it rich, we got to pay him a share. That's all."

"Where is this good friend of yours?" said Slocum.

"Back home."

"Where's home?"

"We come from up in Colorady."

"What part?"

"A farm. Up north."

"It must be great to have a friend like that," said Slocum. "Me? I have to work for every penny I get." Huggy snickered. "What's funny?" Slocum asked.

"What kind of work do you do?" asked Huggy. "Kill people, or something?"

Slocum leaned forward and looked Huggy in the eyes for a long and tense moment. "I do," he said. "Sometimes."

"Mister," said Huggy, "you're making me nervous. I wish you and the sheriff would leave us be. Now, you've done had two drinks out of my bottle, and the sheriff has had one. I think that's enough. Men has a right to drink in private. Who are you?"

"He's Slocum," said Speer.

"Buy your own whiskey," said Barber.

"You're talking mighty tough all of a sudden," Slocum said.

"I ain't going to gunfight with you," said Huggy, "but I reckon I can whip your ass."

"Let's go outside and find out," said Slocum.

8

"Fight! Fight!" someone yelled, and then there was nothing else for it. Huggy and Slocum stood up. Slocum unbuckled his gun belt and handed it to Speer. Huggy unloaded his old Remington six-shooter and gave it to Barber to hold for him. They headed for the door, a whole crowd behind them. By the time Speer and Barber and Stopes got out the door, there was already a circle of bloodthirsty and drunken cowhands, local businessmen, and some women gathered around the two combatants, yelling encouragement and rooting for one or the other. A few bets were made. Speer shoved his way through the crowd to get a good view. Slocum looked over his shoulder at the sheriff.

"This all right with you?" he asked.

"I never did see anything wrong with a good fair fight," said Speer.

As Slocum turned back to face his opponent, Huggy drove a hard right into the side of his head. Slocum staggered back. He would have fallen, but Speer grabbed him under the arms and held him up. Slocum shook his head to drive the cobwebs out. It had been a hell of a blow, especially since it had been unexpected. Huggy danced around, his fists held up in front of his face, partially hiding the

broad grin that had spread over it from dealing the first
blow. Slocum put up his fists and stepped toward Huggy.
He made out like he was about to deliver a roundhouse
right, but instead he kicked Huggy in the shin. Huggy
yowled and bent over to grab at his leg, and when he did,
Slocum delivered his punch. He drove his fist down hard
on the back of Huggy's head. He was surprised that the
man did not go down. He raised a knee hard and fast that
bashed Huggy in the face. Huggy straightened up and staggered back a few steps. Then he roared and ran at Slocum,
his head down. Slocum tried to sidestep, but Huggy ran
into him hard, his head bashing into Slocum's midsection,
and the force of his forward motion carried both men into
the crowd. The crowd yelled with delight and stepped back
to give them room. Slocum pounded Huggy's ribs with
both fists. Nothing seemed to hurt the son of a bitch.

He reached back with both hands, grabbing Huggy's
waistband, and with all his might, he lifted, pulling
Huggy's feet off the ground. Huggy still had Slocum in a
bear hug, and he was holding on, but with his feet off the
ground, his grip was loosening. Slocum spun in a circle,
trying to sling Huggy away from himself. At last Huggy's
grip came loose, and he flew backward through the air,
coming down at last on his face and belly on the hard-
packed dirt of the street. He yowled, more in anger than in
pain. He got himself to his feet and moved in on Slocum,
slowly this time, his fists bobbling in front of his face.

"Come on and fight like a man," he said.

"I'm ready for you," Slocum said.

Huggy swung a wide right, which Slocum blocked with
his left. He drove a right into Huggy's gut. Huggy made a
noise like a whuff, losing his air. He shot out a left, which
grazed Slocum's temple. Slocum shook it off. He was inside the long arms of Huggy now, and he pounded Huggy's
gut with both fists. Huggy was flailing at Slocum's back
and sides with both his arms. Slocum suddenly straight-

ened up, driving the top of his head into Huggy's chin. Huggy straightened then. He staggered back again.

"Goddamn you," he said.

Slocum was circling close to the crowd, and just as he was moving past Barber, Barber stuck out a foot and tripped him. Huggy moved in quick, kicking with both feet, stomping. Speer pulled out his six-shooter and fired into the air, moving into the circle. The crowd shouted in anger, some at the interference of Barber, some at Speer for stopping the fight. Slocum managed to get himself to his feet.

"That's enough," said Speer.

"No, it ain't," said Slocum. Looking around, he said, "Who tripped me?"

Speer nodded toward Barber, and Slocum whirled and slugged Barber on the jaw, knocking him over in the crowd. Barber lay still holding the side of his face and moaning.

"Just keep him out of it," Slocum said. Then without warning, he turned back and drove a straight right into Huggy's nose. He knew he had broken it. It was squishy. Huggy staggered back, both hands at his face. Blood ran through his fingers. He was momentarily blinded.

"Aaahhh," he yelled, holding his face.

Slocum had no mercy. He moved ahead. He drove a hard right to the side of Huggy's head and then a left to the other side. Huggy staggered, then dropped to his knees. He was still holding his face. The blood was still running. Now it was making a pool in the dirt. He was making a noise that sounded like a combination growl and whimper. Slocum looked at him for a moment. Then he turned and walked over to Speer.

"I think the bastard's had enough for now," he said.

"I reckon," said Speer. Then in a louder voice: "All right. Break it up here. It's all over."

Slocum walked to a nearby water trough and ducked his

head in the water. He came up again and washed his face with both hands. Then he pulled the neckerchief from around his neck and used it for a towel. He looked at Speer.

"We never finished our supper," he said.

Back at Brenda's Place, they ordered fresh meals. "We'll pay for both of them," Speer said.

"You already left me some money," said Brenda. "More than enough."

"Oh, yeah. I forgot."

The place was almost cleared out, and by the time Brenda brought them fresh plates, the last customer had left. She poured herself a cup of coffee and sat down with Slocum and Speer.

"So," she said, looking at Slocum's face, "what happened to you? Did it have anything to do with those three men?"

"What three men?" Slocum asked.

"Oh, don't play dumb with me," said Brenda. "You know damn well who I mean."

"Well," said Slocum, a grin slowly spreading across his face, "yeah. It did."

"Slocum whomped up on the big one," said Speer. "If you think Slocum looks bad—"

"I ought to see the other fella?" said Brenda. "Yeah. I know that line too. What started it?"

"Well," said Slocum, "I did, I think."

"You bad man," said Brenda, trying to look like a schoolteacher chastising a small boy. Slocum took a slug of coffee and shrugged.

"We think they're the rustlers," said Speer.

"I know they are," Slocum said.

"We just don't have any proof."

"We know one thing," said Slocum. "I think you'll be glad to hear this too. Ritchie's got nothing to do with it."

"That's great," Brenda said. "How did you find out?"

"Whoever stole this last batch," said Speer, "stole Ritchie cattle and Mix horses. Sold them both at the same place across the line."

"That is good news," Brenda said. "Have you told Dave?"

"We told him," Slocum said.

"And he believed you?"

"He bought it all right. Said he might ought to apologize to Ritchie."

"That's the best news I've heard in a long time," she said. "I like them both. I sure didn't like seeing them at each other's throats all the time."

Back in the saloon, the three partners in crime sat huddled around the remains of their bottle. Huggy held a dirty rag to his nose. He could see again, but he was still in considerable pain. He downed another glass of whiskey. It seemed to help.

"I mean to kill him," he muttered.

"What?" said Barber.

"Who do you mean?" said Stopes. "That Slocum? For licking you?"

"You both know damn well who I mean. Yes. That Slocum. He didn't fight me fair. He hit me in the nose when I warn't expecting it. Damn near blinded me too. I aim to kill the no-good, foolish bastard."

Barber leaned over and whispered, "When?"

"When I'm good and ready," said Huggy. "He won't be expecting it. That's for sure."

"You want us to help you?" asked Stopes.

"You can ride along and watch," said Huggy. "I won't need no help."

"Good," said Stopes. "What about that sheriff? He's the one what shot me."

"I don't give a damn about that," said Huggy. "You can kill him if you want to. Right now I want you to go get another bottle. This one's about done in. We'll take it out to the shack with us. I need to get real drunk tonight."

Out at Mix's ranch, everything was quiet in the main house. Helen had just checked on Dave and found him asleep. She went quietly out of the room and shut the door easily. Carrying a lamp, she walked across the room to a desk that was sitting there. She put the lamp on the desk and slid a drawer open. She fingered through some papers till she found what she was looking for. She took the paper out of the drawer and unfolded it. She glanced at the writing. It was dated some time ago. She thought that she might need to have it dated again, more recently. It should be all right, but she did not want to take any chances. She folded the paper back and replaced it in the drawer. Then she slipped the drawer quietly back in place and turned to walk to her room. Because of his gunshot wound, she had not yet started sleeping with Dave Mix.

Early the next morning, Slocum was riding alone out to Mix's spread. He tried to think of a course of action, but all he could come up with was to keep his eye on Mix's livestock. Maybe the three would try again. If they did, he wanted to be there to catch them red-handed. He had told Speer what he was up to, and then he had ridden out. He was about halfway to the ranch when he saw Helen riding toward him. He halted his horse and waited. When she got up to him, she stopped her horse as well.

"Good morning, Mr. Slocum," she said. "You wouldn't be on your way out to see Dave, would you?"

"I was going out to your ranch," he said. "I want to kind of keep my eye out for those rustlers. I mean to look in on Davey, though, if that's all right."

"Of course it's all right."

Slocum noticed that Helen was all decked out in a riding outfit. She wore a six-gun strapped around her tiny waist and had a Henry rifle in a saddle boot.

"You always ride armed like that?" he asked.

"Of course," she said. "The way things have been around here lately, a girl can't take any chances."

"You think you could shoot your way out of a scrape?"

"I know how to use these," she said.

"Riding into town, are you?"

"I have some errands to take care of," she said. "I'll be coming back shortly."

Slocum tipped his hat, and Helen rode on. He turned in the saddle for a moment and watched her ride. She knew how to handle a horse too. He wondered how good she was with the rifle and six-gun. He turned back around and urged his horse into a trot.

Speer was on the sidewalk when Helen rode into town. He tipped his hat to her as she rode by. "Howdy, Miz Mix," he called out.

"Good morning, Sheriff," she said.

He stood watching as she rode to Lawyer Cal Baker's office and stopped. She dismounted, tied her horse to the hitch rail, and went inside. He decided to walk on over to see Ritchie. It occurred to him, seeing Helen, that neither he nor Slocum had spoken to Ritchie since their visit with Mix. He found Ritchie behind the counter in the hotel. "I'd like a word with you," he said.

"Sure." Ritchie came out from behind the desk and led the way to a table on the other side of the room. He motioned to a chair, and the sheriff sat down. He took off his hat and laid it on the table. Ritchie pulled out a chair on the other side of the table.

"What is it, Thad?" he said.

"Me and Slocum rode out to Mix's spread after we left you with your cattle. Remember? We had Mix's horses to return."

"Sure."

"We went in the house to have a visit with Mix, and we told him that you were in the clear. The same men that stole his horses had stole your cattle. He was sure surprised. Said he guessed he'd been wrong and he'd like to apologize to you. I don't think he's in shape to ride into town any time soon, but I thought you might like to ride out there to see him."

"That's good news, Sheriff," said Ritchie. "Yeah. I'll do just that. Thanks for telling me."

When Speer was gone, Ritchie went into his suite in the hotel. His wife was folding some clothes. "Margaret," he said. She looked up at him and smiled.

"What is it?" she said.

"I'm in the clear with Dave Mix."

"Oh?"

"Thad just stopped by to tell me. You know our cattle that got run off and we went after them and brought them back?"

"Yes?"

"Well, the same men that stole our cattle, I think I told you this, stole some of Dave's horses. Thad and Slocum told Dave. They told him that it couldn't have been me. Thad said that Dave wants to apologize to me. I'm going to ride out there to see him."

"Are you sure that's wise?" Margaret said.

"Why not?"

"He might have just been acting for the benefit of Slocum and the sheriff. It might not be safe for you to go out there."

"But I just told you—"

"You told me about the cattle and his horses. That's what the sheriff and Slocum told him. Did they say anything about his wagons and his store? He might still be holding you at fault for those things. Did you think about that?"

"I'll ask Thad to ride out with me," said Ritchie. "Will that ease your mind?"

"Well, it's better than you riding out alone—if you're determined to go."

Huggy rolled over on the small cot he was using for a bed. He meant to roll over onto his back, but he rolled off the cot, landing with a thud on the floor. He roared as he came awake. Barber and Stopes popped up in their cots.

"What?" shouted Stopes.

"What's wrong?" called out Barber, reaching his gun.

"Goddamn it," said Huggy. "I fell out of the goddamned bed."

"Oh," said Stopes. "Is that all?"

"It didn't do me no good with this shitting hangover," said Huggy. "Barber, get your ass on up and put on some coffee."

"Why me?"

"On account of I'm hurting too bad in my head," Huggy said, "and Stopes's arm is still fucked up. He might spill it all over the place. Go on now."

"I'll have to stoke up the fire," Barber mumbled, putting his gun down and dragging himself out of bed. He walked across the room in his bare feet and long underwear to pick up some sticks of wood.

"You get up too, Stopes," said Huggy. "You ain't laying around in bed while the rest of us is up."

Huggy was sitting on the floor. He was fully dressed, having just passed out on the cot the night before without ever really getting ready for bed. Stopes began dragging himself up.

"I don't see why I can't," he said.

"On account of I got plans," said Huggy, "and I want you both to hear them."

9

When Ritchie got out to Mix's ranch, Slocum was already there, but he was riding the range. Ritchie rode up to the house. It took a while before the front door was answered, and Ritchie was surprised to see that it was Dave Mix who opened it. There was a tense moment that followed before either man spoke. Then Ritchie said, "Dave. What are you doing up and around?"

"I'm getting better all the time," Mix said. "Come in."

Ritchie went inside and Mix motioned to a chair. Ritchie sat down. Mix took a chair across from him and sat slowly with a groan.

"You sure you ought to be up?" asked Ritchie.

"I'm all right," Mix said. "I should have offered you a drink." He started to rise again, but Ritchie stopped him.

"Let me fetch it," he said.

Mix motioned toward a cabinet over against the wall that contained a few bottles and glasses.

"Can I pour you one?" said Ritchie.

"A small brandy," said Mix.

Ritchie went to the cabinet and poured two drinks. He took one to Mix and then sat back down with the other one.

"I came out here to—"

"I know why you came," said Mix. "Slocum and Speer had a talk with me. It seems I owe you an apology. I blamed you for all my troubles, and then you all found three rustlers who had stole from the both of us. I'm sorry, James. I was way too hasty to place the blame."

"If it had been me," said Ritchie, "I'd likely have done just what you did. I ain't holding nothing against you."

"Thanks," said Mix.

"Say, is there anything I can do for you while you're laid up? I can send some hands over, and there's even some things I can do myself if you need any—"

"I'm okay," said Mix. "Charley's got everything well in hand, but thanks for the offer."

Ritchie took a sip of his brandy and thought for a moment. "There is something else I have to say to you, Dave," he said. "We cleared up the rustling all right, but there's still the matter of your wagon and your store. I have to say this even though it'll throw suspicion right back in my way. Dave, there just ain't no reason them three would have to wreck your wagon and burn down your store. There's someone else. There's got to be. I swear to you, Dave, it ain't me, but I sure can't think of anyone else with a reason to do them things to you."

A dark look spread across Mix's face. He had just apologized to Ritchie for suspecting him of all his trouble, and now Ritchie himself had thrown suspicion right back in his direction. It didn't seem likely, though, that he would have done that if he were guilty. Mix was trying to think of something to say when he heard a knock at the door. Again he started to get up, but Ritchie beat him to it, saying, "Sit still, Dave. I'll get it."

He opened the door to Slocum.

"Oh," said Slocum. "I can come back later."

"It's all right," said Ritchie. "Come on in. Me and Dave have just about patched things up all right."

Slocum walked on in the house. "I'm glad to hear that," he said.

"Sit down, Slocum," Mix said.

"You ought to be in bed," Slocum said, taking a seat.

"I already went through all that with him," said Ritchie.

"I'm doing a lot better," said Mix. "What brings you out here?"

"I came out to check over your stock," Slocum said. "Everything looks all right for now. Just thought I'd peek in on you and see how you're doing."

"I appreciate it," said Mix. "Slocum, James here has just brought up something that we seem to have overlooked."

"Yeah?"

"There's still someone else who's after me."

Bart Rowland rode into Hangdog about noon. He was wearing a black suit, black hat, and had a pair of revolvers strapped around his waist. A Henry rifle was snugged down in a saddle boot on the left side of his handsome white stallion. He rode with ease and confidence. He stopped in front of Ritchie's hotel, tied his horse to the rail, and went inside, where he got himself a room. The desk clerk was obviously nervous. Rowland spoke to no one other than the clerk, and that very brusquely. He took his gear up to his room and wasn't seen for the rest of the evening. Rowland was widely known as a gunfighter for hire. As soon as he was gone, the clerk ran around town telling everyone the news. Bart Rowland was in town. Speer stomped around town until Slocum at last rode back in. It was mid-afternoon. He called out to Slocum, and they went to the saloon together and sat down for a drink.

"Bart Rowland just rode in," Speer said.

Slocum's brow wrinkled. "That's interesting," he said.

"What do you think Rowland's business is here in town?" Speer asked.

Slocum shook his head. "It's a puzzle," he said. "If he'd come in earlier, I'd have thought that he came for the same reason as me but for the other side."

"You mean you'd a thought that Ritchie hired him?"

"That would have made sense," Slocum said, "only now it don't look like Ritchie's the one behind the trouble. It looks like those three bums are behind all the running off of livestock, and Ritchie's been a victim just like Mix has."

"Maybe them three just blundered into the middle of all this trouble without knowing what's going on. It could be that Ritchie's been behind the other trouble that Mix has been having all the time, and them rustlers just kind of throwed us off the track."

Slocum took a sip of whiskey. "That could be," he said, "but I kind of doubt it. I don't think Ritchie's involved. There's got to be someone else."

"Slocum," said Speer, obviously exasperated, "there just ain't no one else. Ritchie is the only one who stands to gain a damn thing from Mix's misfortune."

"Someone tried to kill Davey," said Slocum. "I keep thinking about that small boot print where the shooter stood."

"Ah, yeah. I forgot about that," said Speer.

"I passed Helen Lester, uh, Mrs. Mix, on the road when I was riding out to the ranch yesterday," Slocum said. "She was armed to the teeth. Said she could handle a weapon all right."

"Yeah," the sheriff said. "I seen her come into town. She rode straight over to Lawyer Baker's office. When she come back out, she headed back toward the ranch."

"I wonder what that was all about," Slocum said.

"Hell," said Speer, "she was just married. It could a been anything."

"Yeah," said Slocum. "Like a will."

"A will?" said Speer. "Slocum, you ain't thinking what I think you're thinking, are you?" Slocum gave a slight shrug. "A small boot print," said Speer, "a woman who rides around armed and says she can shoot, a wedding, and a will."

"What I'm thinking," said Slocum, "is that I shouldn't have left Davey out there alone with that woman."

"His whole ranch crew is out there," said Speer.

"They ain't in the house," Slocum said. "Speer, I'm riding out there again, and this time I'm staying."

Just then, Bart Rowland walked into the room. He stopped and looked the place over carefully. Then he walked to the bar. The bartender came up quickly to serve him. "Coffee," said Rowland, and he turned and walked to a table and sat with his back to the wall. The bartender rushed a cup of coffee over. "Anything else I can do for you?" he asked.

"Just keep this cup filled," Rowland said.

"Yes, sir," said the barkeep, and he hurried away.

Speer looked at Slocum. He nodded in Rowland's direction. "What about him?" he said.

"Long as he's in town," Slocum said, "he's your worry. If he's here after Davey, he'll have to come out to the ranch."

Slocum finished his drink and left the saloon. Speer stared at Rowland for a moment. Then he took his drink and walked to Rowland's table. He stood looking down at the man. Rowland looked up at him.

"Sheriff, huh?" he said.

"That's right."

"I reckon you want to quiz me up," said Rowland, "so you might as well have a seat."

Speer pulled out a chair and sat across the table from Rowland. "What brings you to town, Rowland?" he asked.

"You know me?"

"I've heard of you."

"Good or bad?"

"Mostly bad. I'm not happy that you're in Hangdog. What brings you here?"

"A job," Rowland said. "The only reason I ever travel."

"You might not know it," Speer said, "but there's a law here against carrying guns in the town limits."

"My job demands that I carry my guns, Sheriff," said Rowland. "Besides that, there's plenty of young toughs who like to be able to say that they killed Bart Rowland. You take my guns and I'm a dead man."

"Who you working for?"

"That's confidential."

"Suppose I guess. Will you tell me if I'm right? Is it Jim Ritchie?"

"I can tell you that it is not Jim Ritchie," Rowland said, "but that's all I can tell you."

"Rowland, wherever you go, someone gets killed."

"I've never killed a man that didn't draw on me first," Rowland said.

"You've egged them on."

"No law against that."

"Look, we've been having trouble in this town. I want to know who brought you here."

"Comet brought me."

"Comet?"

"That's my horse," said Rowland. "He brought me the whole way."

"I want you to know that I'm going to be watching every move you make."

"That's fine with me. I have nothing to hide, except the name of my employer, and I have no reason to see that person until my job is done."

Helen had finished her business in town and was back at the ranch before Slocum got there. She met him at the door. She smiled. "Hello, Slocum," she said. "Come in. You'll find Dave doing much better."

"I know," he said. "I seen him earlier today."

He stepped on in and took off his hat. "Well," said Helen, "if you've come to see him again, you'll find him in the bedroom. I'm afraid he sort of wore himself out today."

"I'd just as soon have a little talk with you first," he said. "In private."

She looked surprised, then shrugged. "Will out on the porch do?"

"It'll do just fine," Slocum said.

"I'll just bring us some coffee."

Helen disappeared into the kitchen for a moment. She returned with a tray containing a coffeepot, a creamer, a sugar bowl, two cups, and two spoons. Slocum opened the door for her, and they stepped out onto the porch. Helen put the tray down on a small table that was standing between two chairs. They both sat down, and Helen poured the coffee. "Cream or sugar?" she asked.

"No, thanks," Slocum said.

Helen doctored her coffee. At last she sat back and looked at Slocum. "Well?" she said.

Slocum felt awkward. He had never done anything quite like this before. Here was the wife of his good friend, and he was going to try to accuse her of attempted murder.

"You know," he said, "that we found out who them rustlers were."

"Yes. I know."

"They had stole cattle from Ritchie and horses from you."

"Yes. I've heard all this. But have you caught them?"

"No. Not yet, but we do know who they are. They won't get away with anymore rustling around here."

"That's good. I think it would actually be better if you caught them, though."

"We will."

"Well, is that all you wanted to talk to me about?"

"No. Right after Davey was shot, me and Speer went down and found where the shooter had stood off the road and waited for him."

"Oh?"

"We found the spot all right. There was an empty shell there, and there was a boot print."

"Really?"

"The print was small."

"And?"

"Like a lady's."

"Indeed," she said. She sipped her coffee. "There are small men, you know. Some have feet as small as any lady."

"I thought about that, and I been watching. I ain't seen no man around here who's that small."

"A lady. Well."

"When I met you on the road earlier, you were well armed. You said that you could shoot."

"Oh, I see what you're getting at," she said. She put her cup down on the table. "You're trying to accuse me of the shooting. Is that it?"

"Well, not exactly. There's just some things that I'd like to have explained. Like what did you ride into town for?"

"I told you, I think. I had some chores."

"According to Speer, you had one chore. You went to a lawyer's office. When you came out, you rode right back out of town."

"That snoopy old sheriff," Helen said. "He's right, of course. I went to see Mr. Baker to have the will changed to reflect the fact that Dave and I were married. He made the necessary changes, and I brought it home for Dave to sign. I'll take it back in the morning for Mr. Baker to take care of. Do you see anything wrong in that?"

"Could be," said Slocum. "You get a will all drawn up and then something happens to Davey, you'd be sitting pretty, wouldn't you?"

"Mr. Slocum," Helen said, "you're overlooking a couple of very significant details."

"What are they?"

"In the first place, with all the trouble Dave's been having, if anything should happen to him, as you put it, I would likely inherit nothing but problems."

"If you're behind all that," Slocum said, "the trouble would quit when you inherited."

"The other thing is, I only had the will fixed up after Davey had been shot. Can you explain that so it makes me look guilty?"

"No," he said. "I can't."

"Slocum," Helen said, "have you told Dave about your suspicions regarding me?"

"I wouldn't tell Davey anything like that," Slocum said. "Not without definite proof."

"Well, I thank you for that."

"It's for his sake, not yours."

"You really do suspect me, don't you?"

"I keep thinking about that small print and about the guns you tote."

"Well," she said, "I don't suppose there's anything I can do about that."

But Slocum had a feeling that she was thinking about something—something other than a worry that he was suspicious of her. He wished that he could read her mind.

10

Slocum rode night herd that night, wishing he could be two places at the same time. He had no idea which ranch the three scum would strike next. For that matter, he had no idea if they would strike that night. They might just decide to clear out, knowing that they were suspected and were likely being watched. There was nothing else for it, though. He had to watch somewhere. Since he was closer to Davey than to Ritchie, he had decided to watch Davey's herd. There were a couple of other riders out, and once or twice in the night he had gone over to the corral to check on the horses. The night was wearing on, and everything was quiet. This night might prove to be a wasted night. He decided to ride out toward the shack on the hill and watch the rustlers rather than the herd. He was moving down the road when he heard the horses coming. Quickly he urged his big horse off the side and into some brush. He waited.

In another moment, three riders came. He waited. They came closer and rode past him. It was the rustlers all right. He waited another moment, then moved out onto the road again to follow them. They rode straight to Davey's ranch. He had been right all along. He followed them at a safe distance. They rode past the main gate and on another mile or so before they stopped. Then Barber dismounted and took something from his saddlebags. He walked to the fence. It was wire cutters. Looking around, he cut the wires, then dragged them out of the way. He had an opening wide enough to drive the whole herd through. Barber remounted, and the three riders went through the opening in the fence. Slocum followed them.

He could hear the herd lowing up ahead. The riders pulled their six-guns and rode a little faster. Drawing closer to the herd, one of the riders took a bead on one of the cowboys. Slocum had no time to waste. He stopped his horse, pulled out his Winchester, cranked a round into the chamber, and raised it to his shoulder. Taking quick but careful aim, he pulled the trigger. The rider jerked in the saddle and slumped forward over his horse's neck. The horse kept running for a distance with the rider flopping around on him. Then the rider slipped off to one side and fell hard. He did not move. Slocum figured he had killed the man.

The other two had stopped riding. He heard a voice say, "Stopes?" Then another shouted, "He's done for. Save yourself." The riders made a hard turn to the left and rode hard. The shot had startled the cattle. They were growing restless, ready to run. Slocum rode fast toward the herd, and when he was close enough to be heard, he called out to the cowboys, who had already drawn their weapons, "Hang onto the herd. I'll get those bastards." He rode after the remaining two rustlers.

Huggy was riding hard toward the hills with Barber not far behind. Slocum tried another shot, but it was wasted, riding hard in the night like that, trying to hit a moving target. He shoved the rifle back into the boot and kept riding. Huggy made it to the hills and he started up a narrow trail. In the midst of large boulders, he stopped. Barber had no choice because of the terrain but to stop behind him.

"What're you doing, Huggy?" Barber said. "That son of a bitch is right behind us."

"We got to ambush him right here," Huggy said. "Get off your horse and get behind that boulder. I'll take this one over here."

Barber dismounted and moved into position behind the boulder that Huggy had indicated. He readied his rifle. Huggy, still on horseback, grabbed the reins of Barber's mount and started riding fast up the hill. Barber turned around to look. He was astonished. Huggy was running away with his horse, leaving him to fight Slocum alone.

"Huggy," he shouted. "You bastard. Come back here."

Huggy was out of sight. Barber turned around again. Now he had no choice except to do what Huggy wanted. He had to ambush Slocum. He had to kill him. That goddamned Huggy, he thought. He cranked a shell into the chamber of his rifle and readied it over the top of the rock waiting for Slocum to appear.

Up ahead, Huggy was riding for his life. That damned Slocum was smarter than he had thought. He was laying for them. Well, Barber would slow him down. Even if Slocum killed Barber, it would take a little time—time enough for Huggy to get away. He thought about riding back to the shack for the supplies, but he decided against that. He had to get away. His only regret was the money in Barber's and Stopes's pockets. He wished that he had that. But he still had his share, and it would last him a little while if he was careful. He reached the top of the hill and turned loose Barber's horse. Then he started down the other side. At the bottom of the hill, he turned in the direction opposite the shack. He was leaving this part of the country forever.

Slocum had seen the outlaws turn up the hill. In the moonlight, he could see the large boulders that flanked the trail going up. He saw it immediately as a good spot for an ambush. He stopped riding and secured his horse to a clump of brush. Then he walked toward the hill. He did not head for the trail. That was where they would be waiting for him. He moved a little left of the trail. When he reached the foot of the hill, he started climbing. It was a little tricky in the dark, making his way among all the rocks. He had to be careful of his footing. He had to be quiet. He listened as he moved, thinking that the horses might make some noise that would give them away, but he heard no noises. Now and then he stopped to listen. It was deathly quiet. He moved on.

Then he spotted something too straight and smooth for nature poking across the top of a boulder. He moved a little closer. At last, he could make out the shape of a man with a rifle. He moved in some more, getting a good location. He slipped the Colt out of his holster. He pointed in the direction of the man. At the same time, he thumbed back the hammer and said in a loud and clear voice, "Drop the rifle and turn around." Barber panicked. He whirled and fired, his shot echoing through the darkness but going wide of its mark. Slocum shot one time. Barber flopped and fell back, draped across the boulder. Slocum moved down cautiously. Barber was dead. But where was the other one?

It took a few minutes for Slocum to realize that the other one was nowhere around, and there were no horses. It was hard to read tracks in the darkness, but he figured that the man had ridden to the top. He went back after his horse, and then he rode the trail to the ridge. There was no sign of the other rider. The sun was beginning to peek up over the far horizon. Slocum looked for tracks. Two horses had come to the top of the hill. One had ridden off along the ridge. The other had gone down the other side. He studied the tracks carefully before deciding that the man he was after had ridden down the hill. He rode after him.

It seemed that the man was riding his horse too hard, Slocum thought. He wouldn't last long at that pace. Slocum took it easy. He would find the man. He had no doubt. The farther he rode, the lower the hills to his right became. Around midmorning, there were no hills left. The man had moved back over onto the road. Slocum kept after him. Eventually, he had to stop and rest his horse. Slocum took the opportunity to have a smoke, lighting one of his good cigars. A little farther down the trail, he stopped again, this time beside a small stream. He allowed the horse to drink and to graze a little. Then he mounted up and continued his way along the road. It wasn't long before the tracks were obliterated by other tracks. Suddenly, the road was more heavily traveled. Slocum figured there must be a settlement of some kind ahead. He rode on.

Then he came to a sign that read, SLAPDASH, 5 MI. He'd never heard of it. He rode on. A wagon came from the opposite direction, and as it passed him by, the driver tipped his hat and said, "Howdy, stranger." Slocum returned the greeting and continued on his way. A couple of cowhands came riding. They greeted Slocum as well. This time he stopped riding. The cowhands did too.

"Say," said Slocum, "did you fellows see a man riding this way about to kill his horse?"

"Sure did," said the one. "A scruffy-looking rascal wearing overhauls."

"That's him," Slocum said.

"You after him?"

"He's a rustler and a killer," said Slocum.

"Yeah. He had that look about him."

"Is there a sheriff in Slapdash?" Slocum asked.

Both cowboys laughed at that. Finally, one of them said, "Mister, Slapdash ain't hardly even a town. It just sprang up here not too long ago. It's got a saloon and a store."

"That's it," the other said.

"Much obliged," Slocum said, and he rode on. The cowhands continued on their way in the opposite direction. Soon Slocum saw Slapdash. Two buildings. That was it. The cowboys had sure told the truth about it. There were several horses on the street, a few people going into or out of the saloon and the store, but it wasn't a big crowd. It wouldn't be hard to locate the man in this place.

Slocum rode up to the saloon. There was just room for one more horse at the hitch rail, and he took it. He looked over the horses tied there, and he spotted the wretched animal that Huggy had been riding. The poor neglected beast was nearly ridden to death. It was caked with sweat, and it stood there panting for breath. Ducking under the rail, he went inside. It was a hastily thrown together building with a false front. Inside the walls were bare boards, the outside light showing here and there through their cracks. It had to be a cold son of a bitch in the winter months, Slocum thought. There was no ceiling, just the bare underside of the roof slats. The bar was thrown together, as were the shelves behind it, which held a myriad of booze bottles. The tables were all mismatched as were the chairs. It was noisy, rowdy inside, what with all the cowhands in for a good time. Slocum stood for a spell just inside the door looking around. A couple of cowhands at the bar glanced at him, a stranger in their midst. At last he spotted Huggy, sitting alone at a table in the far corner of the room, a glass and a bottle on the table in front of him. Slocum headed for that table.

When he had made his way through the roomful of crowded tables about halfway to the corner table, Huggy looked up and spotted him. Fumbling to his feet backward, he tipped over his chair, reaching for the six-gun at his side. Slocum's Colt was out in an instant and leveled at Huggy's gut. Huggy's gun was not halfway out yet. "I wouldn't do that if I was you," Slocum said. Huggy stood still, staring at the barrel of the Colt. He loosened his grip on his own weapon, letting it drop back down, and he spread his arms wide.

"What do you want with me?" he said. "I'm just setting here minding my own business."

The crowd in the room grew quiet, all eyes on Slocum and Huggy.

"I'm taking you back to Hangdog," Slocum said. "Alive or dead. It don't matter to me."

"I'm clean out of that county," said Huggy. "You can't touch me over here."

"I'm no lawman," said Slocum. "Finish your drink. We've got a ride ahead of us."

Huggy looked around the room in desperation. "Say, boys," he said. "You ain't going to let this here stranger come into your town acting like some kind of bounty hunter, are you? Why, he's got nothing on me. I ain't bothered no one in this town. Make him leave me alone."

A cowhand at a nearby table looked up at Slocum. "What do you want him for, mister?" he asked.

"My name's Slocum. No mister."

"All right then, Slocum," said the cowboy. "What do you want with this fellow?"

"He's rustler and a horse thief," Slocum said, "and he killed a cowhand while he was running off cattle."

"I never—"

"He ran off cattle from James Ritchie's ranch and horses from my friend Davey Mix's place. He and his two pards killed a rider called Billy Boy over at Ritchie's."

"Hey," said a cowhand at another table. "I knew Billy Boy. I rode with him at Old Man Farnum's place a couple of seasons back. He was a good hand and a good pard."

"We're all cowhands in here," said someone else. "We got no use for rustlers and horse thiefs."

"Nor no one that kills good cowboys!"

"Wait a minute," Huggy said. "Wait a minute. You got nothing on me but just his word."

The cowboys were too rowdy by this time to listen to what Huggy or anyone else was saying. Billy Boy suddenly became everyone's best friend. They had ridden with him somewhere. They were on their feet, crowding around Huggy, pressing on him and shouting.

"Dirty son of a bitch," someone shouted. "Kill a kid like that."

"I'll just take him back—"

Slocum had started to speak, but no one was listening. He knew what was coming. He backed away out of the crowd and went to the bar. The bartender had joined the crowd shouting insults and threats at Huggy, but he was still behind the bar. Slocum had to yell to get his attention. He called for a drink of whiskey. The bartender put a bottle and a glass hastily on the counter and turned away again, paying no more attention to Slocum. Slocum dug out a coin and put it on the bar. He poured himself a drink and turned it down. Then he poured another. He turned around, but he could no longer see Huggy. The crowd had closed around him. He could hear only a large crowd noise. He could not make out anyone's voice or anything anyone was saying. Then he watched as the crowd seemed to turn all at once. It started moving toward the door. At last he could see several cowboys dragging and pushing Huggy toward the door. The crowd parted just enough to let them through; then it moved along with them. Everyone was shouting, waving fists. When Slocum at last got another glimpse of Huggy, he could see the terror on the man's face. He could see that his mouth was wide open. He was screaming, but his voice could not be heard above the voice of the crowd. As he passed by on his way to the door, he looked at Slocum with a pleading in his eyes. It was ironic. He was pleading with the very man who had followed him to this place to kill him. Slocum turned up the glass and drank his second drink down as the crowd pressed through the door. When everyone was at last outside, Slocum could see that one of the batwing doors had been broken off and was hanging by one hinge. Slocum turned back around as the crowd van-

ished and the noise subsided a bit. The bartender was looking anxiously after them.

"Take care of yourself, mister," he said, ripping off his
apron and hurrying after the excitement. Slocum poured
another drink. He heard a voice behind him.

"You ain't going to watch?"

He turned and saw that one man besides himself was
left in the saloon. The man had the look of a gambler.

"No," said Slocum. "You?"

"I've seen men hanged before," said the gambler. "Have
you?"

"Yeah. A few times. It ain't pretty."

"You came after the fellow," said the gambler.

"Not for this," said Slocum.

"What's the difference?"

Slocum turned his drink up and finished it in one long
swallow. He put the glass down on the counter and turned
to leave. "I guess there ain't any," he said as he walked out
the door. He unwrapped the reins from around the hitching
rail, ducked under the rail, and mounted his horse. He did
not intend to look, but the noises of the crowd were too
much for him to ignore. In spite of himself, he glanced
across the street as he was riding by. He could see the
crowd. He could not see Huggy. They were gathered in
front of the other building in town, a building with a false
front and a board sidewalk in front of it. A roof overhung
the sidewalk, and beams held up the roof. Someone had
gotten a rope over one of the beams. Slocum could see that
it had been pulled tight. It was not very high. As he
watched, he saw Huggy being dragged up by the rope
around his neck. They hadn't bothered putting him on a
horse. They hadn't gone out to find a tree with a high
branch. They had simply strung him up to the nearest thing
that would hold a rope, even though it was not high enough
for a good drop, and they were pulling him off his feet,
slowly and deliberately. Slocum thought that he was too far

away for such a clear view, but he could clearly see Huggy's face, his tongue sticking out, his eyes bulging, horror written bold. Slocum tried to pull his own eyes away from the sickening sight, but his head turned as he rode by. At last, he was far enough down the street that he could no longer see clearly. He could still hear the crowd, though. He kicked his horse in the sides and rode hurriedly away from the town with no law.

A couple of miles out, he slowed his pace. The grisly scene was stamped on his brain, and he could not get it out. Huggy and his two companions had been disgusting, sorry excuses for human beings. Slocum had killed the other two and would have casually shot down Huggy as well, but he would not have sent him away like that. As he rode on his way back to Hangdog, the words of the gambler echoed in his mind. "What's the difference?"

11

Back at the Mix spread, Helen had gotten herself ready for bed. She had just blown out the lamp and was pulling the heavy quilts back on her large four-poster when her door opened, startling her. She turned quickly to see her husband, Dave, standing silhouetted in the doorway. He was wearing a bathrobe. She could not see the expression on his face in the darkness.

"Dave," she said, her voice surprised. "What are you doing in here?"

"It's all right," he said. "You're my wife, ain't you?"

"Yes. Of course. But you're not well. You—"

"I'm well enough to handle you all right," he said.

"Dave, I don't think—"

"You don't have to think," he said, striding across the room to catch her in his arms and plant a firm kiss on her mouth. For an instant, her arms flailed loose. Then they reached around his shoulders to caress him, gently, for she was still worried about his shoulder wound. In another moment, Dave let her go. He pulled off his robe and let it drop to the floor. He had nothing else on.

"Dave," she said.

He started to pull her nightdress down off her shoulders.

"Dave," she protested.

"That's my name," he said. "I like the way it sounds coming out of your mouth."

He caused the nightdress to fall to the floor around her feet. He looked at her for a moment, then reached out to place a hand on each of her firm breasts. Her nipples hardened under his touch.

"Dave," she said, "I don't want you to hurt yourself."

"Then you'd better not struggle," he said, "or you might hurt me."

He pushed her backward slowly until she ran into the bed and lost her balance, falling into a sitting position on the edge of the mattress. He kept coming at her, and she scampered onto the bed, moving to the center. He crawled in on top of her, and he kissed her again. This time, his tongue probed the inside of her mouth. Soon, she responded in kind. They dueled in this manner for a long moment, and then she felt the hardening member between his legs begin to poke at her between her legs.

"Oh," she said, and she reached down with both hands, grasping the rod with one and the heavy balls with the other. She placed the head of the rod against her wet pussy and rubbed it up and down. Then she guided it into her deep hole, and Dave thrust forward and downward with all his might.

"Oh," she said again. "Oh. Oh."

He began pounding with all his might, too eager to worry about her needs. He felt the pressure welling up inside him, and then he spewed forth. In another moment, he rolled off her, lying beside her panting.

"I was afraid it might be too much for you," she said.

"You think so?" he said. He rolled back on her, but this time he moved lower, pressing his face between her thighs, and his tongue darted out and flicked at her tender spot.

"Oh, Dave," she said. "Oh. Oh, yes."

•   •   •

Slocum rode back into Hangdog early the next morning, but it was not so early that Thaddeus Speer was not up and about already. Slocum found the sheriff walking across the street headed for Brenda's Place. He rode up beside the lawman. Speer looked up at him.

"You look like you been riding all night," he said.

"I have," Slocum answered. "You going to breakfast?"

"Yep."

"Mind some company?"

"Nope."

Slocum rode slowly keeping beside Speer till they reached the restaurant. Then he dismounted and slapped the reins of his mount around the hitch rail. He walked inside with Speer. There were a few people in already, the local early birds. Brenda spotted Slocum and Speer and smiled. "I'll be right with you," she said. They took a table, and in another moment, Brenda put coffee on the table in front of them. "What'll you boys have this morning?" she asked.

"Eggs and ham," said Slocum. "Taters, biscuits, and gravy. The works."

"I'll have the same," said Speer.

"I'll have it right out," Brenda said, and she turned and walked away.

"So where the hell've you been?" Speer asked.

"You know those three rustlers?"

"Sure I do."

"I was riding herd at Davey's place when they hit. I dropped one of them right there. The other two took off, and I chased them. Up in the hills, one of them tried to ambush me. I killed him. The other one had run off and left him. I followed him all the way to a little place called Slapdash. Found him having a drink in the saloon. The place was full of cowhands. I pulled on the bastard and told him we was heading back here together, and he appealed to the cowboys for help. So I told them why I was after him. For rustling cattle, stealing horses, and killing a cowboy. They took over then. Wasn't nothing I could do about it."

"What do you mean?"

"They took the son of a bitch out in the street and strung him up."

"Just like that?"

"Just like that."

"I'll be damned."

"Anyhow, that oughta be the end of the rustling problems around here. At least for a while."

Slocum picked up his cup and took a long slurp of coffee. It sure tasted good. He had needed it. He also needed the good food that Brenda was bringing out just then. "Eat it up," she said. "If you're still hungry after that, there's more."

After Brenda was gone again, Speer asked Slocum, "Have you had any more thoughts about that other problem?"

"Who shot Davey?"

"Yeah. And wrecked his wagon and burned his store. That little problem. The thing that brought you to town, if you told me right."

"I keep thinking about that small boot print," Slocum said.

"Oh, that. Yeah."

"I ain't seen a man that little around here."

"You think it was a woman?"

Slocum shrugged.

"It's kinda hard to think about a woman laying in ambush like that and shooting a man down."

"Helen told me she rides every day," Slocum said. "Said she can shoot too."

"Helen and Dave Mix just got hitched," said Speer, astonished at the suggestion.

"I didn't say she done it," Slocum said. "I just used her as an example. If she can ride and shoot like a man, there may be others that can do the same. That's all I'm saying."

"That ain't all you're saying. You suspect her, don't you? You're thinking she might come in here to get that will changed too. And about her not waiting for Dave to heal all up before they got hitched. You're thinking about all that stuff, and you're suspicioning her of trying to kill Dave so she can inherit everything from him. That's what you're thinking, ain't it?"

"Speer," said Slocum, "all I said was I was thinking about that small boot print. You said all the rest of that."

"Yeah, all right, but what about that goddamned gunfighter fellow, that Bart Rowland? What about him?"

"I'd say he was involved some way. Didn't you say that he admitted coming here in someone's employ?"

"That's right, and he won't say who the hell it is either."

"We'd better watch him," said Slocum.

"He said that he ain't got no reason to see his employer till his job's done."

"We need to watch him anyhow," Slocum said.

Helen sat up on the edge of the bed and pulled her nightdress on over her head. As it draped down over her upper body, she said casually to her husband, "Your friend thinks that I'm the one that shot you."

"Who are you talking about?" said Mix.

"That Slocum," she said. "He thinks I shot you."

"He can't think that," said Mix. "You misunderstood something he said."

"I understood him clearly all right," she said. "He found a small boot print at the scene of the shooting, a woman's size."

"That don't prove anything. Hell, I've seen men with feet that small."

"Seen any around here lately?"

"Well, no, but it still don't prove nothing. As far as that goes, you ain't the only woman around here either."

"But who else would have a reason to kill you, darling?"

"What are you talking about?"

"With you dead, I inherit everything. And Slocum did see me out riding, carrying my guns."

Dave Mix sat up quickly and grabbed up his bathrobe. He was walking toward the door as he pulled it on. "I'll straighten out his ass, that son of a bitch," he said.

Charley Hill was riding the range where Mix's land adjoined Ritchie's. Unknown to Hill, not far away on the Ritchie side, Jay Everett was riding the fence. On a knoll not far away, Bart Rowland lay on his belly with a pair of binoculars. He was watching Hill. Hill was riding directly toward him. Rowland waited a space, then set aside his glasses and picked up his rifle, a .38-caliber Volcanic, and took careful aim. He squeezed the trigger. The roar of the shot and the smell of burnt powder filled the air, and a puff of smoke rose up from the spot where Rowland lay. Down below, Hill jerked in his saddle. His head tilted as he looked down at his chest. Then he went limp all over at once and fell back out of the saddle. At his secluded spot on the knoll, Rowland cranked another round into the Volcanic.

Jay Everett heard the shot. He turned his horse and rode toward the noise of the report. The first thing he saw was the loose horse, saddled but riderless. He knew that something was wrong. He pulled the rifle out of his saddle boot and cranked a shell into the chamber. He rode more slowly along the fence, looking to the other side, Mix's side, the side where the loose horse wandered. Then he saw the body. He looked around quickly, but he could see no one. He dismounted and scrambled over the fence, taking his rifle with him. He ran over to the body and recognized it as Charley Hill. He checked it quickly and saw that Charley was gone from this world. Still down on one knee beside the remains of Hill, Everett held his rifle ready and looked around. Still, he could see no one. He did see the tree and brush-covered knoll. Someone could be up there. He was looking at it when he saw the puff of smoke. Then he felt the slug slap into his chest. He sat down hard on his butt and rocked there a moment. Then he fell forward on his face, his legs still doubled up grotesquely beneath him.

Dave Mix stepped out onto his porch and shouted for someone, anyone. A cowhand came running up to the house. "Find Charley for me," Mix said. "And hurry it up. Get someone to saddle me a horse."

"I'll get your horse, Boss," the cowboy said, "but it'll take a while to round up Charley. He rode out to the east range a little while ago."

"Never mind then," said Mix. "Just bring me the horse. I'll ride out after him myself."

Helen stepped out on the porch as the cowboy headed for the corral. "Dave," she said. "What do you think you're doing?"

"I'm going to ride out and get Charley to go to town with me," he said. "I mean to see Slocum and straighten this shit out."

"You're not fit to ride," she said.

"I was fit enough last night, wasn't I?" he said.

"I just think it's too early for you to—"

"Never mind all that," Mix said. "I'm all right."

Just then the cowhand came back leading a fresh, saddled horse. Mix went down off the porch and mounted up. Without another word, he turned the animal and lashed at it, kicking its flanks at the same time. He rode hard and fast away from the house.

Rowland made his way back into Hangdog the back way, avoiding being seen. He left his horse at the livery, with instructions to unsaddle it, rub it down, and feed it well, and special instructions to Dyer to keep his mouth shut. Then he walked the distance to the hotel in the back of the buildings and went inside by the back door. He went quietly up to his room.

Mix rode out to the fence on the east side of his property. It didn't take him long to spot the loose horse, and it wasn't much longer when he came across the two bodies lying there together. He looked around and spotted the other horse on the other side of the fence. He stood over the bodies for a long moment, hat in hand. Then he mounted up and rode back to the house. He found a hand and ordered him to hitch up the wagon and drive it out there. He sent another two cowboys along to gather up the horses and to help load the bodies into the wagon. His instructions were then to take the bodies into town. He sent one cowhand to find Ritchie and inform him of the news. Then he rode toward Hangdog alone.

It was nearly midday by the time Mix reached Hangdog. He stopped in front of the sheriff's office, dismounted, tied his horse to the rail, and went inside. Speer was seated behind his desk. He looked up when Mix walked in.

"Dave," he said, surprise evident in his voice, "I'm surprised to see you up and around so soon."

"I'm all right," said Mix. "I found Charley Hill and Jay Everett dead on my range this morning."

"What?"

"You heard me right. Charley's horse was wandering on my side of the fence, and Jay's on the other side, but both bodies were on my property."

"Did they kill each other?"

"Neither one of their guns had been fired. Someone else got them both."

"Well, was there any evidence of rustling or anything like that?"

"No. Someone just rode out there and shot them both.

That's all. I've sent one of my boys to tell Ritchie about it. I've got another one bringing in the bodies."

"Goddamn," said Speer.

"You know, Slocum said something about someone trying to stir up trouble between me and Ritchie. The only thing I can figure is that this is part of that scheme."

"But who the hell could it be?"

"I don't know, Thad," said Mix, "but it reminds me. Where the hell is that damned Slocum?"

"My guess, this time of day, is that he's over to Brenda's Place. Either that or he will be right soon."

"I'll find him," said Mix, and he turned and walked out the door. As he aimed himself for Brenda's Place, he spotted Slocum walking in that direction. "Hey! Slocum!" he called out.

Slocum stopped and turned to see Mix. He changed his direction and walked to meet Mix. He had a smile on his face, but he soon saw that Mix did not. His own expression turned serious then.

"What is it, Davey?" he said.

"Slocum," said Mix, "you son of a bitch. We need to talk."

12

"Goddamn you, Slocum," said Mix, "what the hell do you mean by accusing my wife of shooting me?"

"Now, Davey, I—"

"What reason could she have for shooting me? For trying to kill me? She's been working her ass off nursing me. If she shot me, why would she do that? Answer me that one, will you?"

"Davey, if you'll just shut up for a minute, I'll try to explain things to you."

"All right. Let me hear it. Let me hear it, you bastard."

"I never accused her. I just said that I found a small boot print, like a woman's, and then I saw her out riding and carrying guns. Then she went into the lawyer's office to see about your will, and—"

"Hell, I was damn near dead. She ought to be checking on that will."

"Yeah. I reckon so. Davey, I—"

"Slocum, you ain't working for me no more. Here." He reached into his pocket and pulled out a roll of bills. Holding them out toward Slocum, he said, "This will cover your expenses, and more. Take it. Come on, take it and ride out of here."

"Davey, I don't want your money. Not till this is all cleared up."

"Take it, goddamn you," said Mix.

When Slocum still kept his hands down at his sides, Mix stuffed the money into Slocum's shirt pocket. "There," he said. "We're finished. There's nothing to keep you around here now."

Mix spun on his heel and walked back toward Speer's office. Slocum stood staring after him, wondering what the hell he should do. He really knew what he should do. He should pack up and ride out, the way Mix told him to. He knew better than to hang around where he wasn't wanted. It would be by far the safest thing for him to do. So why the hell did he not do it? He had gotten into something that wasn't finished, and he hated to ride away from it. He told himself he would just have to stay out of Mix's way. That's all. Avoid Mix but continue to watch, continue to investigate. He could still confide in Speer. He could keep his eye out for that gunfighter Rowland.

Rowland. There was the joker in the deck. Who had brought in that son of a bitch? And for what? To kill Slocum? To heat up the war between Mix and Ritchie? Or was Ritchie really guilty as hell after all, and had he brought Rowland in? Slocum might have thought that the problems were all solved with the killing of the three rustlers if it had not been for the boot print. Just then he saw the wagon come into town with the two bodies. He watched as the wagon drew up in front of Speer's office. In a moment, Speer came out with Davey. He looked at the bodies. Then he gave some instructions, and the wagon pulled on down the street toward the undertaker's parlor. Speer and Mix walked toward Ritchie's hotel. Slocum wondered what was going on, but it was not the time to question Speer, not with Mix in his company. He walked over to Brenda's Place and ordered some coffee.

Brenda wasn't busy. She poured two cups and sat down

with Slocum. "You're wearing a long face," she said. "Something bothering you?"

"Yeah," said Slocum. "Davey's run me out of town."

"What for? I thought you two were good friends."

"Yeah. I did too. But I quizzed up his wife about his shooting. She must have told him."

"You mean you—"

"I saw a woman's boot print where the shooter was standing," Slocum said. "Then I saw her in riding gear packing irons. I questioned her. Davey didn't take too kindly to that."

"Well, he just married her. You can't expect him to."

"That was another thing. She got hitched up to him before he was well enough to stand up. She was in an awful hurry. Then she hurried into town to get the will changed."

"Hmm. That is suspicious-looking."

"Don't say that to Davey," Slocum warned. "He'll run you out of town too."

"I'll keep it to myself," she said.

"Have you seen that Rowland around?"

"He came in here once," she said. "That's all. He's a mean-looking jasper. But his feet are bigger than a woman's."

"He showed up after Davey got shot too. No. I don't think he shot Davey, but I think that whoever it is stirring up trouble likely brought him in. I'd sure like to know what he's up to."

"If I hear anything, I'll let you know."

"I appreciate it," said Slocum.

Slocum lifted his coffee cup for a long slurp, and just then Speer came walking in. He went straight to the table where Slocum and Brenda were sitting and pulled out a chair.

"Mind if I join you?" he said, sitting down.

Slocum said, "What if I said yes?"

Brenda said, "Not at all. You want some coffee?"

"Sure."

She got up and went for another cup, bringing the pot back with her.

"Jay Everett and Charley Hill have been killed," said Speer. "Shot to death in the same spot. Right by the fence line between Ritchie's and Mix's."

"Oh, no," said Brenda.

Slocum took out a cigar and lit it, sending smoke spiraling toward the ceiling.

"Any evidence?" he asked.

"I ain't been out to the scene yet," said Speer, "but Mix says that it looks like one man done the shooting."

"But why would anyone shoot Dave's and James's foremen?" asked Brenda. "Both of them?"

"Stirring up the trouble," said Slocum.

"Yeah," said Speer. "Say, Dave just told me that he fired you."

"That's right."

"How come?"

Slocum told the tale again about his questioning of Helen. "She told on me, I guess," he concluded.

"What are you going to do?"

"Stick around," said Slocum. "I feel like I've got unfinished business here."

"I'm glad to hear you say that. We still have that Rowland to worry about."

"Do you think maybe he killed those two?" asked Brenda.

"That'd be my guess," Slocum said. "Sheriff, you want to ride out and look over the scene?"

"I was hoping you'd offer to go with me," said Speer.

Slocum drained his coffee cup. "Then let's go for a ride. Thanks for the coffee, Brenda, and the company."

In his apartment in the hotel, James Ritchie sat deep in thought. His wife, Margaret, brought him a drink and then sat down across the room from him. "It had to be Mix," she said. "Who else could it be?"

"Why would he kill Charley Hill?"

"To cover his tracks maybe," she said. "He might have figured that anyone would ask that question. Who else could have a reason to keep the trouble going between you two?"

Ritchie took a drink, then shook his head. "I don't know, Margaret. I just can't think of anyone who could gain anything from it."

"You said that he patched things up with you. Well, that was just an act. That's all. He's still blaming you for all his trouble, and now he's trying to get even."

"I just can't hardly think that Dave would murder those two men like that. He just never seemed like he could do that."

"This whole business has made him crazy. You're too trusting, James. You always have been. What are you going to do about it?"

"I don't know. There's no proof. I can't do anything without proof."

"You can do what he did," she said.

Slocum and Speer had no trouble finding the spot of the murders. Mix had told Speer where to look, and there were still bloodstains on the ground. They dismounted and tied their horses to the fence. They studied the blood for a time. "Dave said they was both laying right here," said Speer. "Together. Only Everett's horse was on the other side of the fence."

"Maybe Everett heard the shot and came over to investigate," Slocum said. "Maybe they weren't together at all."

"Maybe," Speer agreed.

Slocum stood up and stared at the knoll off a short distance. Speer looked at him. "Are you thinking the shooter was up there?" he asked.

"It's a likely place," Slocum said. "Let's take a look."

They got their horses and rode over to the knoll. They hesitated only a moment, and then they rode to the top. They dismounted and started to look around. In a minute, Slocum found the spot where the shooter had been lying on the ground.

"Grass is still mashed down," he said. "He was on his belly right here. He must have picked up his spent cartridges, though."

"Yeah. I sure don't see any around."

They found where the shooter's horse had been left, but there were no clear prints of any kind in the deep grass.

"Not much to go on," Speer said.

"Just my gut feeling," said Slocum. "I vote for Rowland on this one."

"Could be."

"Most likely."

Back in town, Slocum and Speer went to the hotel and found Rowland's room. Speer knocked on the door. A voice from inside the room said, "Who is it?"

"It's me, the sheriff. Speer."

"Come on in," said the voice. "The door ain't locked."

Speer opened the door and stepped inside, followed by Slocum. Rowland was stretched out on the bed, his six-gun in his right hand, cocked.

"What are you doing with that damn gun?" Speer demanded.

Rowland let the hammer down and shoved the gun back into the holster hanging on the bedpost. He grinned.

"I had to make sure it was really you," he said. "Being careless is a good way to get dead."

"Then I'd be real careful if I was you," said Slocum.

"I'm always careful."

"You been out riding lately?" Speer asked.

"I've been right here in this room."

"I'll check on that," Speer said.

"Check away. My employer has given me no instructions as yet."

"I'm wondering if you've been riding out to Mix's ranch," Speer said. "Maybe found a little knoll close to the fence line between Mix's and Ritchie's. Maybe laid up there a while waiting for someone to come riding by."

"No. I never," said Rowland.

Slocum was looking around the room, and he spotted the rifle. He walked over close to where it was leaning against the wall in a corner of the room.

"That's a nice-looking Henry," he said. "Do you mind if I take a look at it?"

"Help yourself," Rowland said.

Slocum picked up the rifle. He looked it over carefully. He sniffed it. "It's just been cleaned," he said.

"A man who don't take care of his weapons might get dead," Rowland said.

Slocum put the rifle back down. "Yeah," he said. "He might get shot or he might get hanged."

"What's that supposed to mean?"

"Nothing. Just talk."

"Rowland," said Speer, "I'm asking you again just who the hell you're working for. Are you going to tell me?"

"I can't tell you," Rowland said. "That's part of the deal."

"Were you hired to kill someone?"

"I never kill except in self-defense."

"If there are witnesses," said Slocum.

"Are you trying to raise my hackles, Slocum?" Rowland said. "Because if you are, you're wasting your time and your energy. It ain't going to work."

"What if I was to just call you out?"

Rowland grinned again. "One of us would have to draw first," he said. "It wouldn't be me. You might get yourself arrested for murder."

"It might just be worth it."

"Never mind that kind of talk, Slocum," said Speer. "I don't want any gunfights around here. But I don't want any more killings either."

"Has someone been killed?" Rowland asked. "Since I been in town?"

"Two men," said Speer. "Ritchie's foreman and Mix's foreman. They was shot down out on Mix's range this morning early."

"And you think I done it," said Rowland. He grinned again. Slocum wanted to wipe the grin off his damn silly face. "Well, Sheriff, if you get any evidence against me, come and see me about it then. In the meantime, I'd appreciate it if you'd leave me be."

"You've got to come out of this room sometime, Rowland," said Slocum. "When you do, we'll meet up."

"I'll be looking forward to that. By the way, it's kind of strange seeing you with the sheriff. Ain't you and me in the same line of work?"

"I doubt it," said Slocum.

"I've heard of you. You hire out your gun. I heard that you were here as a hired gun. Someone brought you in before I come along. I heard it was Dave Mix."

"Dave's an old friend of mine," Slocum said. "He wrote me he was having some trouble, and I came here to see if I could help out. He didn't hire me to kill anyone."

"I heard you killed three men already since you been here."

"Rustlers," said Speer. "I know all about that."

"Did you have proof?"

"We did."

"Would it have held up in a courtroom?"

"We'll never know that, will we?" said Speer. "I think it would have, though."

"We're in the same business, Slocum, me and you," said Rowland, and he grinned again. Each time he grinned, his grin seemed wider. Slocum turned and walked out of the room. Speer walked to the door, but he stood in the doorway for a moment. He turned and looked back at Rowland.

"I'll be watching your every move," he said. "If you spit on the sidewalk, your ass will be in jail."

"I'll be real careful what I do while I'm in your town, Sheriff," Rowland said.

Speer walked on out in the hall and joined Slocum. They walked down the hallway without speaking, and then they started down the stairs. "I think you were right, Slocum," Speer said.

"About what?"

"He's the guilty one all right."

"We got to find a way to prove it, though," Slocum said.

"We need to find out who hired him," said the sheriff.

"Hell," Slocum said. "Why don't you just let me call him out?"

13

Bart Rowland got up one morning, packed his belongings, went to the livery for his horse, and rode out of town. Slocum and Speer both saw him go. He rode in the wrong direction to be headed for either Mix's or Ritchie's spread.

"He's leaving town," said Speer.

"I don't believe it," Slocum said. "I mean to follow him."

"If you get yourself into any shooting scrape," said Speer, "just make sure it's out away from my jurisdiction."

Slocum grinned at Speer. "I wouldn't do anything to piss you off, Sheriff," he said. He followed in Rowland's steps, going to the livery for his horse. He was in no hurry, for he did not want Rowland to know that he was being followed. In a few minutes, he was riding out of town. Speer watched him go too. He wondered what would happen when the two gunfighters met up with one another. He hoped that Slocum would survive it. When Slocum was out of sight, Speer walked on over to Brenda's Place. He found himself a table and sat down. Brenda was right over with a cup of coffee.

"Thanks," Speer said.

"Anything else for you?" Brenda asked.

"Just coffee," Speer said.

Brenda looked around the room. Her few customers all seemed contented for the moment, so she sat down at the table with the sheriff. "Something wrong?" she asked.

"Just this whole business," Speer said. "Those two men getting killed like that. Slocum is damn sure that Rowland is behind it, but Rowland rode out of town this morning—all packed up like he's leaving for good. He was headed north. Slocum followed him. Could be a showdown, I guess. Slocum asked me how come I didn't just let him call Rowland out. Maybe I should have. Hell, I just don't know."

"I think Slocum can handle himself all right," Brenda said.

"Yeah? But we ain't seen Rowland in action. He's got a hell of a reputation."

"Well," she said, "all we can do is wait and see what happens."

"I keep thinking there ought to be something else I could be doing. There's trouble around. Bad trouble, and I'm the sheriff. I hate just sitting and waiting for something else to happen."

Dave Mix rode up to Ritchie's hotel just as Ritchie walked out the front door. Mix dismounted and slapped the reins around the rail. Ritchie could tell by the look on his face that Mix had not come in for a friendly visit. He saw the six-gun strapped around Mix's waist. He stopped on the sidewalk and waited for Mix to make the first move.

"Ritchie," Mix said, "let's have it out right now."

"What are you talking about, Dave?"

"A showdown. Just you and me. Then it will be over once and for all, one way or the other. Come on. You wearing a gun?"

Ritchie opened his coat to show that he was not.

"Well, go back in and get one," Mix said. "I'll wait for you right here. Go on."

Ritchie turned and went back inside the hotel. It was only a short wait for Mix. Ritchie came back out. He was not wearing his coat, and he had a six-gun belted on.

"Margaret tried to tell me it was you behind all this trouble," Ritchie said. "I didn't believe her."

"You're talking bullshit," said Mix. "It all started when you had my cattle rustled and my wagons wrecked. My store burned down."

"That was those three men that Slocum killed."

"They done some of the rustling all right, but they didn't do all that other stuff. They didn't shoot me from ambush either."

"How do you know that?"

"Slocum found a boot print. A woman's," Mix said.

"Hell," said Ritchie, "that could've been left there at any time by anyone."

"That's enough jawing. Go for your gun."

"I'm surprised you didn't send your hired gun Slocum to do the job."

"Slocum don't work that way," said Mix. "Besides that, I fired him. Where's your gunfighter?"

"I don't have any gunfighter," Ritchie said.

"Come on now. That Rowland you brought in. Where's he at?"

"He rode out of town this morning. And I never brought him in. I don't even know him."

"Are you going to go for your gun?"

Speer came walking up just then. "What the hell's going on here?" he demanded.

"Stay out of this, Thad," said Mix. "This is between me and Ritchie. It always has been. I mean to see it finished right here and now."

Speer walked straight toward Mix.

"Keep out of this," said Mix.

Speer reached up for the brim of his hat seeming exasperated. Suddenly he whipped the hat off his head and slapped Mix hard across the face, at the same time reaching down and pulling out Mix's shooter. He stepped back quick and leveled the gun at Mix.

"Damn you," said Mix.

Speer turned around and walked up to Ritchie, holding out his left hand. "I'll take yours too," he said. Ritchie pulled out the gun with two fingers and held it out for Speer. The sheriff took it, and with a gun in each hand he stepped back so he could face both men. "Any more trouble out of you two, and I'll lock both of you up. You hear me?" No one answered. "Do you understand what I'm saying?"

"I can get another gun," Mix said.

"If you do, you're going to jail," said Speer. "I ain't fooling with you. You come back in town packing any kind of gun, I'll throw your ass in jail. Now get on out of here."

Mix grudgingly got back on his horse and rode out of town fast. Speer turned on Ritchie.

"The same thing goes for you, James. I see you packing iron, you're going to jail."

He turned and walked toward his office. Ritchie went back into the hotel.

Slocum followed Rowland all day. When Rowland stopped and camped for the night, Slocum did the same. He was up early the next morning. Rowland had already broken camp and started riding. Slocum followed. Again, Rowland rode all day with Slocum on his trail. Slocum was beginning to wonder if Speer had been right and Rowland was leaving the area for good. Then he saw that they were coming to a town. Slocum let Rowland ride on in, and he found a place where he could hide and watch. It was late in the day, and he made himself another camp. He was up on a rise, and he had a good view of the small town. He did not want to confront Rowland yet. He wanted to find out what he was up to. He would hide and watch.

It was far into the night. Slocum had decided that nothing was going to happen until morning. He had rolled out his blanket and was sleeping soundly when he felt someone kick him in the side. He woke up and started to reach for his gun, but he was stopped by the sound of a rifle chambering a shell. He squinted in the darkness, and he recognized the form of Bart Rowland standing over him. He glanced around slowly. There were four other men. So that's what Rowland had been up to—recruiting more men. Getting reinforcements.

"Stand up slow," said Rowland.

Slocum tossed the blanket aside and stood. A man behind him took his Colt. Another picked up his Winchester.

"I never heard of you needing to bring extra men along to do your killing," Slocum said.

"I ain't going to kill you, Slocum. No one's paid me to kill you."

"What then?"

"You'll find out soon enough. Beebe, get his boots. Rat's Ass, fetch his horse over here and saddle it up."

The man called Rat's Ass went for the horse and saddle. Rowland never took his eyes off Slocum.

"You should've let me alone, Slocum," he said. "A little professional courtesy goes a long ways."

"You're messing with a friend of mine," Slocum said.

"When it comes to business, there ain't no such thing as friends. Cowley, you and Naylor tie him to that tree over yonder. Tie him good and tight."

The two men shoved Slocum toward the tree and pulled his arms back and around it. Then they tied his hands. They tied his feet and legs by wrapping rope around him and the tree.

"Put one around his neck too," Rowland said. "Not too tight. I don't want him killed, just immobilized."

When Cowley and Naylor had finished, Slocum could hardly move. If he tipped his head too much, he would choke. They had done a good job of it. Rowland relaxed his guard. He turned to the one he had called Rat's Ass. "Pack all of his stuff on the horse," he said. "Guns and boots too." When they were ready to go, Rowland suddenly swung his rifle butt, smacking Slocum a good one to the side of the head. Slocum felt the blood trickling down the side of his face and on down his neck. Then Rowland whacked him a couple of times in the ribs. Slocum's head sagged, and the rope choked him. He had to lift his head again. "Let's go, boys," Rowland said. "Bring his horse along."

They all mounted up, Rat's Ass leading Slocum's horse, and they started to ride off. Rowland was in the rear. He hesitated and looked down at Slocum. "You should have stayed out of it, Slocum," he said. "You know, you could die up here, all trussed up like that. No food. No water. No weapons. It gets cold at night too."

He kicked his horse in the sides and rode on after his four recruits. Slocum sucked in air. His ribs hurt. Rowland might have cracked a couple of them. His head hurt like hell. He was in a very uncomfortable position. He couldn't sleep. His head would drop, and he would be choked. He figured that Rowland had been right. He could die right there. It wasn't a way he had ever figured he would go. A gunfight maybe, a knife in the ribs in a saloon brawl, but not this. He had been a fool to let Rowland and those scummy bastards slip up on him like that. He wondered just how long Rowland had been aware of him. As soon as he rode out of Hangdog maybe. Maybe he had been planning this all along. Slocum had sure been suckered all right, and it might well be for the last time.

Stumpy Morgan was out of a job. He was riding toward Hangdog, and if he found nothing there, he had heard that there might be jobs to be had around a little place on a ways called Slapdash. He was a good cowpuncher, and he shouldn't have any problems if he could just come across some spread where they were a little short-handed. He was riding along whistling an old tune when he saw the stray horse. He rode up to it casually. It was saddled and packed. There was a rifle in the boot, and a six-gun in a holster was hanging across the saddle horn. Then he noticed that a pair of boots had been stuffed halfway into the saddlebags. It was sure peculiar. Carefully, he reached for the reins. He did not want to spook the creature. He got hold of the reins all right, and he talked to the horse in soothing tones. At the same time, he looked around for any sign of the rider.

The country around was pretty flat, mostly prairie. Stumpy could see for a good ways in most directions, and he did not see anyone. Of course, if the rider was hurt, he might be lying flat in tall grass. But there were the boots. That didn't make any sense. There was a slight rise in the landscape a little ways back. Stumpy had passed it a short while ago. It was one spot where he couldn't see too well. He decided to ride back to it and look up on top. Even if he didn't find anyone up there, he should be able to look over the prairie all around from a better vantage point. Leading the horse, he headed back. Even though he had a destination in mind, he kept watching all around as he rode. A man down like that could be anywhere.

He didn't see anything before he reached the rise. He stopped for a moment studying it. Picking the most likely-looking route, he headed up. He had just reached the top of the rise when he saw the man tied to the tree. He hurried over and quickly dismounted. The man looked dead, his head was hanging forward, and there was a rope tied tight around his neck. Stumpy lifted the head, and the man coughed. His eyes opened slowly, and he looked at Stumpy. "Just hang on a bit more, pard," Stumpy said. "I'll get you loose from there." He pulled a bowie knife out of a sheath at his belt, and he sawed at the rope around Slocum's neck. When he had severed it, Slocum let his head drop again, this time without choking. Stumpy sliced the ropes that bound Slocum's arms around the tree, and finally he knelt to cut the ropes that bound Slocum's bootless feet. Freed from the tree, Slocum nearly collapsed. Stumpy caught him and helped him to sit down.

"You ain't a rustler, are you?" Stumpy asked. "That's a mighty peculiar way to hang a man."

Slocum shook his head. He couldn't make any words come out of his mouth. Stumpy ran over to his horse and got the canteen, bringing it back to Slocum and offering a drink. Slocum drank greedily. Stumpy took it back, saying, "I think that's about enough. Take it easy. Say. I don't know how long you been there, but could you use some coffee and something to eat?"

Slocum nodded, and Stumpy got busy building a fire. Soon, he had some grub cooking and coffee boiling. Checking it all, he walked over to Slocum's horse and fetched the boots and the Colt back to Slocum. Holding them out toward Slocum, he said, "I'd bet these are yours." Slocum nodded again and reached out for the items. He put them on the ground beside himself. Soon, Stumpy handed Slocum a plate, and Slocum ate like he hadn't eaten in a week. Stumpy gave him a cup of steaming coffee, and Slocum drank it down like it was cold. Stumpy poured him some more, and he shoveled more food on the plate. When Slocum at last finished eating, he sat with a cup of coffee. He had some strength back. He was rested, and his throat was feeling some better.

"I want to thank you," he said.

"Name's Stumpy. Stumpy Morgan."

"Thanks, Stumpy. I'm Slocum."

"Say, if you don't think it's none of my business, just say so, but I got to ask. How the hell did you wind up like that anyhow?"

Slocum told the whole story to Stumpy, beginning with the letter he had received from Mix sometime back.

"Damn," Stumpy said. "So who do you think hired this Rowland?"

"I got no idea," Slocum said.

"You going back for him?"

"What do you think?"

"You don't seem like no quitter to me."

"I'm going back," Slocum said, "but I don't mean to face him with this right off. He'd just deny it, and if I killed him, the sheriff would be after me. I'm going back and I'm going to do what I was doing all along. I mean to watch him and catch him at something. Figure out who he's working for. Then I'll get him. One way or another."

"You said your friend was pissed off at you. Told you to get out of town."

"I don't need his pay," Slocum said. "This is all on my own now."

"Yeah," Stumpy said. "I can see why. But you got five men to deal with now, and you still don't know just who to blame for all this trouble. It sounds to me like you've set yourself up for one hell of a job. Them ain't good odds."

"The sheriff's a good man," Slocum said. "He just needs proof before he can do anything. But if I get the proof and it comes to a showdown, he'll be with me."

"That's a big if."

"I'll get it, though," Slocum said. "Either that or I'll get myself killed."

"It means that much to you? Even after you got fired?"

"It does now."

"Slocum?"

"Yeah?"

"You want a pard in this deal?"

14

Slocum and Stumpy did not head back right away. They both decided that Slocum needed a little time to let the sore wear off his ribs and get the circulation working right in his arms and legs again. To encourage the circulation, Slocum did what he could to help Stumpy with gathering firewood, building fires, boiling coffee, and cooking up grub. Slocum practiced pulling his Colt too. After another day and a night, Slocum felt like he was about as good as new. He was ready to ride. He and Stumpy saddled up their horses, rolled up their blankets, and mounted up. They rode along in silence for quite a spell. In the time they had spent in camp, Slocum had already filled Stumpy in on all the details of what had been going on back at Hangdog. He was a little surprised that Stumpy had elected to ride along with him and jump right into the fight, but he had seen stranger things happen. He liked Stumpy right away, and he guessed that Stumpy had liked him too. Sometimes things happen that way. Men hit it off right from the first. This seemed to be one of those times.

"What are your plans, Slocum?" Stumpy asked. "Just hide and watch?"

"I reckon," said Slocum. "At least for a spell. If I can't

catch ole Rowland in the act or figure out who he's working for, I might just have to prod him into a fight."

"Well, you just give me the word," Stumpy said. "I'll be right alongside of you."

When Rowland and his four new recruits came riding into Hangdog, Speer saw them. He felt a moment of panic. He had not yet seen Slocum, and it bothered him that the man Slocum had ridden after had come back to town first, and with reinforcements. He stepped out into the street in front of the horses. Rowland called a halt.

"What can I do for you, Sheriff?" he said.

"Where the hell is Slocum?" said Speer.

"Slocum? How should I know?"

"Don't play games with me, Rowland. Slocum followed you out of town. I know it, and you do too."

"It's the first I've heard of it. I haven't seen him. Maybe he got lost along the way."

"You're lying to me, but—"

"But you can't prove it," said Rowland.

"Well, you're right about that—for now. Who're this sorry-looking bunch with you?"

"Why don't we just kill him for talking like that about us?" said Rat's Ass.

"You could try it," said Speer, talking more bravely than he felt.

"Just hold on, boys," said Rowland. "We ain't starting no trouble here. Remember?"

"So answer my damn question," demanded the sheriff.

"What question?" Rowland asked. Then he added, "Oh, yeah. These here are my associates. It seems that the job I took on was a little too big for me to handle alone. Don't worry, though. Like I said, we're not starting any trouble in your little town."

"I wish to hell I had a reason to slap your ass in jail."

Rowland grinned his wide grin. "I'll just bet you do," he said.

"It's been too long," Speer said to Brenda. "Way too damn long." They were sitting in her place during a slow time of the day. There were no other customers in the place. "Rowland came back yesterday. And Slocum left out of here following Rowland. Brenda, I'm scared to death that no-good gunfighting bastard killed him and left him out there somewhere."

"Give it a little more time, Thad," Brenda said. "There could be some other explanation."

"I don't know what the hell it could be."

"I don't either," said Brenda, "but something. There just has to be some other explanation. I'm not giving up hope. Not yet."

"Margaret," said Ritchie, pacing the floor in his apartment in the hotel, "I've got to get my hands on a gun and go out there after Mix. He came to town to kill me, and if I wait around too long, he'll try it again. The next time he might not be so open about it. I can't just sit around here cooped up in this place. I have to be able to move around."

Margaret walked to him and put her arms around him. "Take it easy, James," she said. "Be a little more patient. I don't want you to go out and get yourself killed. Something will happen soon. I'm sure of it." She led him to the couch and made him sit down. Then she sat beside him. "I don't want to lose you. So don't go riding off half-cocked. You hear me? You understand?"

Mix was fuming too. "We'd have shot it out if Speer had kept his nose out of our business. If he hadn't come along when he did, it would all be over now. Either Ritchie or me would be dead."

"And what if it was you?" Helen said. "What am I supposed to do if you get yourself killed? Run this place by myself? With all the trouble we've been having? Don't be a fool, Dave. If you get killed, it's all over. We've lost. I can't handle it alone. I'd have to sell out for whatever price I could get and then move on."

"Where would you go?" Mix said.

"I don't know. Back East, I guess."

"All right," he said. "I won't go riding into town after him again. I'll stay out here and keep my eyes open. But I'm keeping a gun handy just in case."

It was the next day when Slocum and Stumpy came riding into town. Slocum led Stumpy straight to the sheriff's office. They tied their horses and went inside. Speer almost jumped out of his chair.

"Slocum!" he shouted. He came running around his desk to grab Slocum's hand and pump it like crazy. "Slocum. Goddamn it. I've never been so relieved to see anyone in my whole life. Damn. I was afraid that Rowland had killed you when I saw him ride in and you hadn't showed up."

"He damn near did," said Slocum. "He would have if Stumpy here hadn't come along."

"Stumpy?" said Speer. "Glad to meet you." Now he pumped Stumpy's hand. "Any friend of Slocum's is a friend of mine. You sure done us a favor if you saved Slocum's bacon." He looked back at Slocum. "What the hell happened?"

"I guess I let my guard down," said Slocum, and he told Speer the tale of how Rowland and his new crew had slipped up on him in the night and how they had left him for a slow death. "I'd likely be buzzard bait already if Stumpy hadn't come along."

"I wouldn't have if them bastards hadn't turned his horse loose," Stumpy said.

"Rowland bring them four into town with him?" Slocum asked.

"Yeah. They're with him. Let's go arrest the bunch of them right now."

"We can't do that," Slocum said. "It's just my word against the five of theirs."

"Well, there's Stumpy."

"I'm afraid I never seen them," Stumpy said. "I just come along and found Slocum."

"Damn it," said Speer. "You're right, I guess. If we was to take them to trial, they'd just get off. It'd be a waste of time and money. Damn."

"We'll get them," Slocum said. "Don't fret about that."

"All right then," said Speer. "Let's go see Brenda. She's been awful worried about you too."

"Let's go."

They were walking toward Brenda's Place when Rowland and his four cronies came out the front door of the hotel. They were obviously startled when they saw Slocum. They stopped still. Beebe and Rat's Ass were about to go for their guns, but Rowland stopped them. Slocum, Speer, and Stumpy changed their direction and strolled over to face them. Rowland grinned and tipped his hat.

"Howdy, Slocum," he said. "It's good to see you. The sheriff here has been mighty worried about you. He even thought that I might have killed you out on the road. I'm glad you made it back safe and sound."

"I'm sure you are," said Slocum. "I just wanted to make sure you saw that I made it back all right. And I want you to know, all five of you shit-asses, that I mean to kill each one of you deader'n a buzzard-picked goat."

"Sheriff," said Rowland, "you're a witness. You and this cowhand here. You both heard Slocum threaten me and my associates here."

Speer looked at Stumpy. "Did you hear anything?" he asked.

"I must have something in my ears," said Stumpy. "I didn't hear a damn thing."

"Come on," said Slocum. "We've got places to go."

They turned and walked away from the gang and headed on toward Brenda's Place. The five outlaws stared after them for a while.

"There's three of them and five of us," said Rat's Ass.

"Don't get cocky," said Rowland. "I don't know nothing about that cowboy, but Slocum's top-notch. And that sheriff, from what I hear, ain't no slouch."

"You don't think we could take them?" asked Zeb Naylor.

"I'd rather not try it out in the open," said Rowland. "We'll just wait for our chance."

Slocum and his two companions walked into Brenda's Place and found her cleaning the tables, getting ready for the supper crowd that would start coming in soon. When she saw Slocum, she ran to throw her arms around him and hug him close and tight. At last, she turned loose and stepped back, a little embarrassed. She looked at Speer. "I told you," she said. "Didn't I?"

"You sure did, and I'm damn glad you were right."

"Brenda," said Slocum, "I want you to meet the reason I'm here at all. This is Stumpy. He sure enough saved me."

"Thank you, Stumpy," she said, holding out her hand. Stumpy took off his hat with his left hand and shook her hand with his right.

"It was my pleasure, ma'am," he said.

"Well," Brenda said, wiping her hands on her apron and looking around the empty room, "find yourselves a table and have a seat. I'm going to fix the three of you the best meal you've ever had."

"Your crowd'll be coming in soon," said Speer.

"Yeah? Well, you're the first."

It was three o'clock in the morning when Rowland led his gang out of Hangdog. They had sneaked their horses out of the livery never waking old Morgan Dyer. If everything went according to Rowland's plans, no one would ever know they had left town. Rowland's employer had told him that it was about time for a showdown, and he meant to get it instigated this night. They rode slow and easy until they were out of town. Then Rowland whipped up his mount, and the other four followed his lead. They rode hard and fast out to Mix's ranch. There they slowed down again. They moved slowly onto Mix's range and rode until they spotted the cattle. There were a couple of cowhands riding slowly around the herd. One of them was singing a song.

"All right, boys," said Rowland, his voice low, "let's take them."

Beebe and Cowley slipped out their rifles. They each cranked a shell into the chamber and raised the rifle, taking careful aim. Beebe fired first, but only an instant before Cowley. They lowered their rifles and watched as the two cowboys fell from their horses.

"Come on," said Rowland. They moved in on the herd, which had already started stamping around nervously. It didn't take any effort at all to get them moving. They only had to turn them in the right direction. Rowland rode fast ahead of the others. He rode until he came to the fence that separated the Mix range from the Ritchie range. Leaping out of his saddle, he ran to the fence with his wire cutters and snapped the four strands of barbed wire. He hurried back to his horse and mounted up again. Paying out his lariat, he swung a loop and roped a post. Wrapping the end of his rope around his saddle horn, he nudged his horse and pulled up the fence post. He kept going until he had pulled up several of them and dragged them and the wire off out of the way. And just in time. Here came his four riders chasing the herd. They drove the herd through the opening he had created and onto Ritchie range. When all the cattle were through the fence, Rowland yelped at his men, and they turned around and rode back through to the Mix side. They kept riding until they were at the ranch house. Rowland pointed toward the big barn off to their left, and Cowley and Zeb Naylor headed for it. At the same time, Rowland, Beebe, and Rat's Ass moved toward the house. Rowland watched the barn until he saw the beginnings of flame creeping up one side. Then he drew his sidearm and fired through a window of the house. Beebe and Rat's Ass did the same. Cowley and Naylor were riding hard to join them. As soon as they drew close, Rowland yelled, "Let's get out of here." The five men rode hard back toward town.

It wasn't long before the hands at Mix's place were roused up by the sounds of the fire. They grabbed their boots and ran for buckets. When Mix and Helen came out on the porch to see what was going on, all hands were busy fighting the fire. Mix ran to help them. He could tell, though, that it was a lost cause. The best they could do would be to keep the flames from spreading. The horses in the nearby corral were already spooked. Helen ran to the corral and pulled loose the pole that served as a gate. Then she went into the corral and shooed the frightened horses through the gate. The horses ran wild. The hands would have to round them up later. Right now, there was the fire to worry about.

They fought the blaze for most of the night. When the fire was finally out, the barn was a total loss. As tired as they were, some of the men went out looking for the horses. A few of the horses were close enough that they were rounded up shortly. The men who got them saddled them up and rode out looking for the rest. Helen went in the house and put some coffee on. They would be wanting it. The sun was peeking over the far horizon when one of the riders came back in and found Dave Mix surveying the damage.

"Boss," he said, "there's more bad news."

"What the hell is it?" said Mix.

"I found Hal and Hembree out on the range. They was shot dead. The cattle's been drove off. I follered the trail. They went through a hole in the fence over to Ritchie's place. The wire'd been cut."

"Ritchie!" said Mix.

"That's where they went."

"Cattle drove off, barn burned, fence cut, and two more dead men," Mix said. "Well, by God, Helen's not talking me out of it this time." He turned and stomped his way back to the house.

Slocum was asleep, but Stumpy could not sleep. He was sitting up in Slocum's hotel room. He thought about going downstairs to see if the saloon was still open, but he was afraid that he might wake Slocum getting dressed and out the door. He stood up and walked sneakily over to the window to look idly out, and he saw Rowland and his four hoot owls riding slowly into town. He watched as they made their way to the livery and took their horses inside. He kept watching. Soon Rowland peered from around the front door and looked up and down the street. He stepped out and motioned with his arm, and the other four came out behind him. Glancing around as they moved, the five skulking men made their way to the hotel. When they came up to the front door, Stumpy lost sight of them.

He wondered what they had been up to. It had to be something no good. They had been out riding in the middle of the night and had come back into town sneaking all the way. He decided to wake Slocum, and he stepped over to the bed and joustled him by the shoulder. Slocum opened his eyes.

"What is it?" he asked.

"Them five, Rowland and the others, they just this minute come sneaking back into town. They'd been out riding somewhere."

Slocum got up and pulled his clothes on in a hurry. He and Stumpy left the room and went down the stairs. As they went out of the hotel by the front door, Stumpy said, "Where are we going?"

"Livery," said Slocum.

Inside the livery, they found the five horses. They were lathery. They had been ridden hard. Just then old Dyer came walking up hoisting his galluses up over his shoulders.

"Slocum?" he said. "What can I do for you?"

"Check these horses," Slocum said. "These five men have been out somewhere, and you're a witness."

15

Mix and his wife rode into Hangdog with a couple of cowboys. There was safety in numbers, and Helen had insisted on it. They did not go after Ritchie, however. They went straight to the sheriff's office. And they did not go packing guns. Not after Speer's threat to Mix the last time they met. Their six-guns were stashed in their saddlebags, though. After hitching their horses at the rail in front, the four riders all went into the office. Speer was there, sitting behind his desk. He looked up when they came in.

"Dave, Miz Mix, boys, how are you all? What can I do for you today?"

"You can go after Ritchie," said Mix.

"Hush up, Dave," said Helen. "Let me handle this." Mix turned away sulking. "Sheriff Speer," she continued, "last night we were hit again. Someone cut our fence and drove our cattle onto Ritchie's place. They killed two of our riders. And they burned our barn. We're lucky that our house didn't catch fire."

"Did you see anyone?"

"Of course not," Mix snapped.

"I'll have to ride out and investigate," said Speer.

"And—" Mix started to say.

"And have a talk with Ritchie," said Speer.

"I think you'd ought to throw his ass in jail," said Mix.

"Dave," said Helen, "let the sheriff do his job."

"Thank you, ma'am," said Speer.

"If he would," mumbled Mix.

"Is there anything else you can tell me about what happened last night?" Speer asked.

"I'm afraid not," Helen said. "We woke up to the noise of the fire. There was no one around by then."

One of the cowboys said, "I found the bodies and seen where the cattle was drove through the fence. I rode back to the house to tell the boss."

"All right," said Speer. "You all go on back home now and leave this to me."

"Come on," Helen said. Mix and the two cowboys followed her back out to the horses, where they mounted up and rode back toward the ranch. Speer strapped on his six-gun, took a rifle out of the cabinet, put his hat on his head, and walked out the door. He was walking toward the livery when he spotted Slocum and Stumpy.

"Hey," he called out. "You boys come along with me."

"Where we headed?" said Slocum.

"Mix's place," said Speer. "They got hit last night."

Slocum and Stumpy looked at each other. Then they fell in step with the sheriff headed for the livery. "In that case," Slocum said, "Stumpy's got something to tell you too."

"What's that?"

"Rowland and his rowdies come riding back into town in the wee hours this morning," Stumpy said.

"We went down to the livery and checked their horses," said Slocum. "They'd been rode hard."

"There's got to be a connection there," Speer said. "Let's go on out to Mix's place and look it over before we do anything else, though."

"All right."

• • •

Rowland and his cronies were still asleep when Slocum, Stumpy, and the sheriff rode out of town. They'd had a long and hard night. Rowland was the first one to wake up. He washed his face in the bowl on the table and took his time getting dressed. His four bad men were asleep on the floor. He was about to pull on his boots, but first he gave Beebe a swift kick in the butt. Beebe sprang up. "What?" he said. "What?"

"Wake up the others and get dressed," said Rowland. "You don't need to sleep away the whole damn day."

"We got something to do?"

"I just told you. Wake the others up."

They were soon all dressed and ready to go, and Rowland said, "Go over to the eating place and order me up a breakfast."

"Just you?" said Rat's Ass.

"No," said Rowland. "Order for all of us. I've got to go have a brief meeting with our boss, but I'll be right along."

"What do you want?" said Rat's Ass.

"The usual."

Rowland waited till the four were out of sight. Then he started on his way.

Beebe, Rat's Ass, Cowley, and Zeb Naylor all walked over to Brenda's Place. They walked in and found a table and sat down. Rat's Ass pounded on the table with his fist. Brenda came out and made her way to their table. "What'll it be, boys?" she said.

"How about a little kiss?" said Rat's Ass.

"What do you want to eat?" Brenda said in an icy voice.

Beebe ordered five breakfasts, and Brenda looked at him questioningly. "There's another feller coming along," he said. Brenda walked away to get the meals started. Then she brought out five cups and a coffeepot and poured the cups full. She turned to walk back to the kitchen, but Rat's Ass grabbed her by the arm. "Let me go," she said.

"Now, pretty little gal," said Rat's Ass, "you and me will get along just fine."

"Your breakfasts will all burn up," she said.

"Let her go," said Beebe.

Rat's Ass loosened his grip, and Brenda stomped away. Beebe leaned toward Rat's Ass. "Rowland'll kick your ass good," he said. "He told us not to start no trouble in town. Remember?"

"Hell," said Rat's Ass. "I wasn't starting no trouble. Just talking to my sweetheart. She liked it too."

"Didn't hardly look that way to me," Beebe said.

"Shit. You just don't know nothing about women."

"I know enough to tell when one's pissed off."

The door opened and Rowland walked in. He made his way to the table and sat down. Picking up his coffee cup, he gave it a tentative sip. It was still hot enough. "You get our food ordered?" he asked.

"Yeah," said Beebe. Rat's Ass gave Beebe a look, but Beebe paid it no mind. He'd let it go if Rat's Ass would. About then, Brenda came back with the plates. She distributed them all around.

"Anything else?" she asked.

Rat's Ass grinned up at her. "Just what we talked about before," he said.

She turned quickly and walked away. Rowland watched her go. Then he looked at Rat's Ass. "What was that all about?" he asked.

"Aw, nothing," said Rat's Ass. "I just asked her for a little kiss. That's all."

"Grabbed onto her too," said Cowley.

"Pissed her off good," added Zeb Naylor.

"We'll talk about this later," said Rowland. "Eat up."

They were about finished with their meals and had not had any refills of coffee. Rowland got up and walked to the kitchen door. He rapped gently on the door. "Ma'am," he called out softly. "Ma'am, could we please have some more coffee?" Brenda jerked the door open and gave him a hard look. "I'm sorry about that fella's behavior," he said. "It won't happen again. Could we have some refills? Please?"

"Okay," she said. She refilled their cups and went back in the kitchen. Rowland took out a slim cigar and lit it. They drank their coffee. Rowland's cigar was about half smoked.

Rat's Ass said, "I want some more coffee."

"You don't need no more," said Rowland. "Let's go."

He stood up, and the other four did too. Rowland dug into his pocket for some money. Brenda was still in the kitchen. He told the others to go on outside, and he went back to the kitchen door and rapped again. When Brenda opened the door, he handed her the cash.

"I'll have to get your change," she said.

"You keep it," Rowland said. "Maybe it'll make up a little bit for my friend's bad manners."

He tipped his hat, turned, and headed for the front door. Brenda stood staring at him until he was out of sight.

Outside, Rowland walked past the other four. "Come on," he said. They followed him between two buildings and around to the alley. He stopped walking abruptly, turned, waited till Rat's Ass was just about up to him, then smashed Rat's Ass in the side of the head with a hard and unexpected right cross. Rat's Ass sprawled backward in the dirt. His right hand went to his hurt jaw, and he looked up at Rowland with wide eyes.

"Get up," Rowland said. "Get up."

Beebe and Cowley reached down and hefted Rat's Ass to his feet. Rowland hit him again and again sent him sprawling. This time, Rat's Ass's hand went for his six-gun, but before he could budge it, Rowland had his own gun out, cocked and aimed at Rat's Ass's gut.

"Try it," Rowland said.

Rat's Ass slowly moved his hand away from his weapon.

"I told you to behave yourself in this town," said Rowland, "didn't I?"

"Well, yeah, but—"

"Shut up. Didn't I?"

"Yeah."

"I ain't going to say it again," said Rowland. "Next time, I'll kill you."

Rat's Ass struggled to his feet. "There won't be no next time, Boss," he said. Without another word, Rowland turned and walked back toward the main street. The others followed him. Rat's Ass mumbled, "He damn near broke my fucking jaw."

Out at Mix's ranch, Slocum, Stumpy, and the sheriff examined the ground around the cut fence. Slocum found a boot print there where it might have been made by the man who cut the fence. It wasn't particularly distinctive, though. He dug his fingers into the ground. It was soft. He examined the dirt and grass and wrapped a bit of it up in his bandanna, poking it into his pocket. They rode over onto Ritchie's land and found the stolen cattle. Then they backtracked and rode to the house. The barn was a total loss. They found the hoofprints of several horses, but they couldn't be sure just how many, and they found more boot prints, but there were so many prints made by the cowhands trying to put out the fire that none of them were of any use. While they were looking at the ruins of the barn, Mix came out of the house. He stomped over to the ash heap near the sheriff, and he pointed a finger at Slocum.

"I don't want him on my place," he said. "He's not working for me anymore. I told him to ride on out of here."

"You can fire a man," said Speer, "but you can't make him leave the country."

"Well, I don't want him on my property."

"He's working with me," the sheriff said.

"That's all right," said Slocum. "I'm just leaving."

"So are we all," said Speer. "Let's go."

They mounted up and rode away, leaving the fuming Mix coughing in their dust. On the ride back to town, they talked about what they had found. "Do you think Ritchie had anything to do with it?" Speer asked.

"No," said Slocum. "It's too obvious to anyone except Davey. He's so damn mad, he can't think straight."

"That's kind of what I was thinking too," Speer said.

"Someone's trying to stir up a range war?" Stumpy said.

"That's what it looks like," said Slocum.

"I bet it's that Rowland," Stumpy said.

"Almost for sure," said Slocum, "but he's working for someone."

"We got to find out who that is," said Speer. "What if I was to throw Rowland in jail and we was to watch his boys? They don't appear to be too bright. They might lead us to someone."

"They might not know who it is," Slocum said. "He brought them in later."

"Yeah. That's right."

"Well, I don't know about you boys," said Stumpy, "but I'm about to starve to death."

"I'm kind of hungry myself," Slocum said.

"We'll hit Brenda's Place soon as we get back to town," Speer said.

They rode straight to Brenda's and went inside. Brenda was leaning over with a dustpan and a broom. The sheriff and Stumpy went to a table, but Slocum stood watching Brenda. She straightened up and turned. Slocum said, "What you doing there?"

"Oh, nothing much," Brenda said. "Some customer came in here with dirty boots. That's all. I'll be right with you." She headed for a trash bin, but Slocum stopped her.

"Let me see that," he said.

She handed him the dustpan. "Whatever for?" she said.

Slocum put the pan on a table and reached into his pocket for his bandanna. He placed the bandanna on the table beside the dustpan and unwrapped it.

"Who was sitting here last?" Slocum asked.

"It was that Rowland and his—"

"Associates, he calls them," said Speer.

"Come over here, Sheriff," said Slocum.

Speer got up and walked over to stand beside Slocum. He looked down at the table.

"What do you say?" Slocum asked.

Stumpy walked over to take a look as well.

"It's the same stuff," said Speer.

"I'd say so," Stumpy added.

"This here," said Slocum, pointing to the dustpan, "is what Brenda just swept up. She said that Rowland and his crew was the last ones to sit here."

"I heard her say that," said Speer.

"Me too," Stumpy added.

"And this here," said Slocum, indicating the dirt in his bandanna, "I picked up out at the fence at Mix's place. Right there by the boot print. Where the man cut the fence."

"So Rowland cut the fence," said Stumpy.

"We knew that already," said Speer.

"But this is proof," Slocum said. "Brenda, do you have a napkin or something I can have?"

She fetched one over right quick, and Slocum poured the dirt out of the dustpan into it. He wrapped up both small bunches of dirt and handed them to Speer. "There's your evidence, Sheriff," he said. "And us three here are your witnesses."

Speer stuffed the two bundles into his vest pockets. "So what do we do now?" he said. "Arrest them?"

"Let's think about that while we eat," Slocum said.

"I like the sound of that," said Stumpy.

"I'll get you some grub," said Brenda, and she walked

into the kitchen. The three men sat down at a table. In a minute, Brenda brought out the coffee. Then she went back to the kitchen to tend to the cooking. Slocum lifted his cup and took a long sip of hot coffee.

"Our problem is still the same," he said. "If we arrest Rowland and them, we still don't know who hired them."

"You're right about that," said Speer. "I sure hate to keep letting that son of a bitch run around loose, though."

"Me too," Slocum said. "I just can't think of any other way."

"You all don't think that Rowland, if he was sitting in a jail cell, might not tell on his boss?" Stumpy asked.

"He might," said Slocum.

"But I don't think so," Speer said.

"Neither do I," said Slocum. "He just don't seem like the type to tell."

16

Rat's Ass had been pouting ever since Rowland had bashed his face. He did not believe that he deserved such treatment. Rowland had not as yet paid the four men anything, and Rat's Ass felt cheated. At the same time, he did not want to confront Rowland about this issue. He decided at last that he could get another job as easily as he had gotten this one. He was going to leave. He wanted nothing more to do with Rowland. He wanted to kill Rowland, but he didn't have the guts, and he admitted that fact to himself. He waited until night when Rowland and the others were asleep. Slowly and carefully, he stood up from the floor. He picked up his gun belt and his blanket roll. Throwing the blanket roll over his shoulder, he picked up his boots. Tiptoeing to the door, he stood there for a moment figuring out how to open it. He laid the gun belt carefully over his other shoulder, turned the key in the lock, opened the door just enough, and went through. In the hallway, he shut the door again as quietly as possible. Then he crept down the hallway to the top of the stairs. There he buckled the gun belt around his waist. He sat down on the top step and pulled on his boots. Standing up, he walked down the stairs.

There was no one at the desk. He strolled across the

lobby to the front door and went out onto the street. He was walking toward the livery when Slocum spotted him from his hotel room window. Slocum thought about waking Stumpy, but decided against it. He continued watching until Rat's Ass came out of the livery leading his horse. He mounted up and rode north out of town. Slocum wondered what was going on. This was the first time any of the bunch had ventured out alone. He pulled on his boots, strapped on his Colt, and put his hat on his head. He was about to go out the door when Stumpy rolled over with a moan. Seeing that Slocum was headed out, Stumpy sat upright.

"Going somewhere?" he asked.

"One of that bunch just rode out of town by himself," said Slocum. "I aim to follow him."

"Want me to ride along?"

"I'd rather you keep watching to see if the others do anything."

Stumpy stood up and stretched. He yawned. "All right," he said. "I'll do'er. You be careful, though, pard. You know what happened the last time you follered one of them bastards."

Slocum grinned. "I'll watch myself," he said. He went out the door and headed for the livery. Soon he was riding after Rat's Ass.

Rat's Ass had gotten about three miles out of Hangdog when he stopped his horse. He reached down into one of his saddlebags and pulled out a bottle of whiskey. He uncorked the bottle and took a long slug. Then he replaced the cork, dropped the bottle into his coat pocket, and started riding again. That son of a bitch Rowland, he was thinking. He promised us all kinds of money and a hell of a good time, and look how he done me. Son of a bitch.

Slocum was in no hurry to catch Rat's Ass. He was curious about where Rat's Ass might be going and what he was up to. He was not headed toward either Ritchie's or Mix's place. Slocum wondered what other kind of errand Rowland might have sent him on. He did not want to surprise Rat's Ass too soon to find out, though, so he continued, curious, following Rat's Ass's tracks.

Up ahead, Rat's Ass stopped beside the road. He took another slug of whiskey, and he took a leak. He felt like he was well enough out of Hangdog that he did not have to worry any longer about Rowland and the others. In the first place, even if they knew which way he had gone, they wouldn't likely catch up with him. They probably wouldn't even try. Good riddance, they would say. He hoped that they would get into a hell of a fight and Rowland would be wishing he'd treated Rat's Ass better because he would need another gun. That would serve him right, the son of a bitch. He decided that he could spare the time to rest a spell. His horse could use a little rest too. He looked around for a likely spot, and then he sat down on the ground. He took another drink. Pretty soon he stretched out on his back. Soon, in spite of his intentions, he was fast asleep.

Slocum rode up on the sleeping Rat's Ass. He thought about kicking the bastard awake, but he decided against it. Keeping his eyes on the sleeping wretch, Slocum dismounted and took the saddle off his horse. He staked it out to let it graze. He noticed that Rat's Ass's mount was still saddled. It wasn't the horse's fault that it had a shit-ass for a rider. Slocum unsaddled it. He kept watching Rat's Ass, but Rat's Ass still snored. Slocum gathered up some wood and built a small fire. It would be daylight soon, and coffee would be damn good. The morning was just a bit chilly. When he had the fire going, he put together a pot of coffee and set it on to boil. Then he sat down, facing Rat's Ass, and lit a cigar. He would wait for the coffee to be ready and for Rat's Ass to wake up. He wondered if he should walk over there and take the six-gun out of the holster at Rat's Ass's side. He decided he should.

He stood up and walked quietly over to the side of the sleeping outlaw. Rat's Ass snuffled and shifted his weight, but he did not open his eyes. Slocum reached down and carefully slipped the gun out of the holster. He walked back to his place beside the fire. The coffee was about ready, and he poured himself a cup. It was hot, and it was good. He was still curious about Rat's Ass's intentions. What he was doing just didn't make any sense to Slocum. He sipped his coffee and put down the cup. It was a wonder that the fire, the cigar, and the coffee had not wakened Rat's Ass. The fire was crackling, and the aromas of cigar and coffee were powerful. He stared at Rat's Ass through clouds of circling cigar smoke.

At last Rat's Ass stirred. He rolled over on his side. He rolled back and stretched his arms, moaning out loud at the same time. He rubbed his eyes with his fists. Finally, he sat up and looked around. When he saw Slocum and the fire, he slapped at his side. He looked down in disbelief at the empty holster. Slocum held up the confiscated weapon.

"You looking for this?" he asked.

"What—what the hell?" said Rat's Ass.

Slocum took a sip of coffee. Then he picked up a second cup. "Have some coffee," he said. He poured the cup full, reached across the fire, and set it on the ground. Cautiously, Rat's Ass got onto his hands and knees and reached the cup. Taking it up, he retreated back to his original spot. He held the cup in both hands and took a sip, staring wide-eyed at Slocum the whole time. He took another sip. Then he pulled the whiskey bottle out of his coat pocket and poured some into the coffee. He started to put the bottle back into his pocket, but he hesitated. He held it out toward Slocum.

"You want some?" he asked.

"No, thanks," Slocum said.

Rat's Ass took another sip. "You meaning to do me like we done you?" he asked.

"What do you mean?" Slocum said.

"You know, tie me to a tree. Leave me without no guns, no horse, no boots."

"Kick in your ribs and bash your face?"

"Yeah. Like that."

"That ain't my style," Slocum said. "If I was to leave you tied to a tree, it would be hanging by your neck from a branch." He looked around. "I don't see a real good branch nearby."

"No," said Rat's Ass. "There ain't none. I done looked."

"Why would you have been looking for a hanging tree?"

"I wasn't. I was just, you know, checking my surroundings."

"I want to know something," Slocum said.

"Yeah? What's that?"

"Where you headed?"

"I'm just leaving," said Rat's Ass. "I quit Rowland."

"Oh? How come?"

"He pissed me off, the son of a bitch."

"Tell me about it."

"He knocked me on my ass. Twice. Right in front of the other fellas. Son of a bitch."

"What did he do that for?" Slocum asked.

Rat's Ass grinned, showing his broken and yellow teeth. "You know that little ole gal that cooks back there in Hangdog?"

"I know her," said Slocum.

"All I done was to just ask her for a kiss. That's all. She didn't mind none either. If I hadn't a had them others with me, I bet she'd a give me a lot more than just a kiss."

You dirty little shit-face, Slocum thought, but he didn't say it. Instead, he said, "And he hit you just for that?"

"That's all. That was it."

"So you ran out on him?"

"I sure as hell did."

"Did you help him steal those cattle and kill those two cowboys? Burn the barn?"

Rat's Ass shifted nervously. "I don't know what you're talking about."

"What was your job with Rowland?"

"I—I don't know nothing."

"Who hired Rowland?"

"He never told us that. I don't know."

"Well, now, I don't know," Slocum said, "but it seems to me that if you helped a man do some rustling and killing and barn burning, he might not want you running around loose. He might come after you to kill you to make sure you keep your mouth shut."

"I mean to get far away from here," Rat's Ass said.

"So you did help him with that job?"

"I didn't say that. I just mean to get away. I don't like that damn Rowland."

"Scared of him, are you?"

"No. I ain't scared," Rat's Ass lied. "I just don't want to be around him no more. Nor them others neither. I don't need them. Maybe they did kill them cowboys and steal them cattle. Maybe they burned the barn too. They could've done it."

"All five of you were seen riding back into town that night," Slocum said. "Where had you been?"

"Who says he seen us? You can't prove that. Maybe he seen four riders and not five. It being dark like that. Maybe he made a mistake."

"I don't think so."

"You thinking it don't make it so."

Slocum took a sip of coffee and put the cup down again. He puffed on his cigar. "You want some more coffee?" he asked.

Rat's Ass sneaked back to where he had picked up the cup and put it on the ground. Slocum reached over and refilled it, and Rat's Ass sneaked back for it and back to his place. He sipped it down a little and poured some more whiskey into the cup.

"Look," said Slocum, "I'm trying to make this easy on you. All I want is a little information."

"If I tell you what you want to know, will you let me go?"

"Not if you killed those cowboys."

"I never."

"You'll get a fair trial."

"Rowland and them'd kill me first."

"Not if they're locked up in jail."

"Yeah? Well, what if they didn't get locked up? What if they was to kill you and the sheriff? And I had told on them? They'd come after me then."

"You've been lying to me," Slocum said. "If you didn't help do that job, then Rowland wouldn't have any reason to come after you. Would he?"

"You're putting words into my mouth."

Slocum heaved a heavy sigh and tossed what was left of his cigar into the fire. Then he tossed the contents of his cup. He dropped the cup on the ground and stood up, leaving Rat's Ass's gun lying on the ground. He stepped around the fire moving toward Rat's Ass. Rat's Ass scooted back.

"What're you going to do?" he asked.

"I want to know who hired Rowland," Slocum said, "and I want to know who did that job at Mix's ranch. I mean to find out one way or another."

"I tell you, I don't know nothing."

Slocum grabbed Rat's Ass by the shirtfront and dragged him to his feet. He slapped him hard across the face. He slapped him again.

"Leave me go," whined Rat's Ass. "Leave me go."

He raised a knee, trying to drive it into Slocum's crotch, but Slocum blocked it with his leg. It pissed him off, though, and he slugged Rat's Ass, causing him to sprawl back in the dirt.

"Get up, you little shit," he said.

Rat's Ass turned onto his hands and knees, and he clutched a handful of grass and dirt in his right hand. He stood up and flung the dirt and grass into Slocum's face. Slocum's hands went to his face, rubbing his eyes. He staggered back a few steps, and Rat's Ass ran at him, throwing his arms around Slocum and shoving him back onto the ground. They rolled over two or three times. At last, Slocum wound up on top of Rat's Ass, and he grabbed the shirtfront once more and stood up, dragging Rat's Ass with him. Rat's Ass swung wildly with both fists, most of his blows landing on Slocum's back. Slocum delivered a hard uppercut to Rat's Ass's jaw that caused him to stagger back.

"Talk to me," Slocum said.

"I can't. I don't know nothing."

"Tell me what I want to know, and we can stop this bullshit here."

"I don't know nothing," Rat's Ass screamed, and he ran at Slocum again with his arms flailing. Slocum stepped aside and flung Rat's Ass as he passed him by, sending him sprawling on his face. Rat's Ass put both hands on the ground to push himself up to his feet, and he saw his gun lying there beside him. He hesitated a moment. Then he reached for the gun and spun around, cocking back the hammer as he turned. He was sitting on the ground as he pointed the gun at Slocum. Slocum flung himself to one side pulling his Colt as he did so, and he squeezed the trigger. The report was loud in the still night. The smell of gunpowder replaced the other odors that had filled the air. Rat's Ass jerked as the bullet tore into his sternum. His hand went limp, and his gun fell. He looked down at his chest and saw the spreading blood.

"Oh," he said. "Oh, God."

He fell back and lay still. Slocum walked over to him and knelt on one knee. He picked up the gun and tossed it aside. Then he holstered his Colt.

"You shouldn't have tried that," he said.

"Can you get me to a doctor?" Rat's Ass asked in a weak voice.

Slocum shook his head. "There's not time enough," he said. "You'd be dead a mile down the road."

"I'm dying then."

"Yep."

"We was trying to start a range war," said Rat's Ass. "I don't know how come. I don't know who hired Rowland. We did steal them cattle. Well, we run them onto the other fella's range, and we burned the barn. It was Beebe and Cowley what killed the cowboys."

"Do you know anything about what Rowland did before he brought you four in on the game?"

"No. I told you everything I know," said Rat's Ass. "Can you get me my bottle out of my pocket?"

Slocum reached into Rat's Ass's pocket and pulled out the bottle. Miraculously, it was unbroken. He uncorked it and held it toward Rat's Ass, but just as he did, Rat's Ass died. Slocum tossed the bottle aside. He rolled Rat's Ass up in his blanket. Then he caught up both horses and saddled them. He tossed Rat's Ass across his saddle, mounted his own horse, and headed back toward Hangdog, leading the horse that was carrying the grisly load. He had learned everything he needed to know about Rowland except who had hired him. There was still that nagging problem.

17

Rowland woke up and stretched. He got out of the bed and walked over to the table with the bowl and pitcher of water on it, stepping over the bodies on the floor as he did so. He poured some water into the bowl and sloshed some on his face, reached for the towel, and dabbed his face dry. Stepping back over the bodies on his way to his britches, he noticed that something was missing. He looked down at the sleeping forms of Beebe, Cowley, and Zeb Naylor.

"What the fuck?" he roared.

He kicked Beebe in the ass. Beebe sprang up.

"What?" he said. "What is it?"

Rowland was kicking Cowley and Naylor by then. Both of them sat up, Cowley rubbing his eyes and Naylor looking stupidly at Rowland with wide eyes.

"Where the hell is Rat's Ass?" Rowland demanded.

The three men on the floor looked around as if they might find the missing Rat's Ass.

"I don't see him, Boss," said Beebe.

"Well, no shit, you don't see him," said Rowland. "He ain't here. I didn't ask you if you seen him. I said, where the hell is he at?"

"I don't know," Zeb Naylor said. "We all went to sleep last night at the same time."

"He was right there," said Cowley, pointing to a spot on the floor.

"Well, he ain't there now," said Rowland.

"He ain't there," said Cowley.

"He must a got up and gone somewhere," said Beebe. Cowley stood up and walked around the room. "His stuff's all gone," he said.

"He's run out on us," said Naylor.

"Well, by God," said Rowland, "we can't have that."

"No," said Beebe.

"We sure as hell can't have that," said Rowland. "You three dumb asses get up and get dressed. We're going to find the little chickenshit."

"We going to have breakfast first?" Cowley asked.

"There ain't time for that," said Rowland. "Hurry it up."

"One of them four bums that Rowland brought in rode out of town last night," Stumpy was saying. "Slocum rode after him."

He was sitting in Brenda's Place with Speer having breakfast. They had a table by the front window, which gave Stumpy a clear view of the front door of the hotel. He was still on duty, still watching for any movement from the others.

"What was Slocum riding after him for?" Speer asked. "Just to see what he was up to?"

"He didn't jaw about it much," Stumpy said, "but that was about the way it sounded to me."

"Well, by God," said Speer, "I hope he's careful. You know what happened the last time he rode out after someone."

"I reminded him of that," Stumpy said.

"I wonder if we had ought to ride out after him."

"He told me to keep an eye on them others. They ain't come out of the hotel yet."

"What could that one have been up to?" Speer said.

"That's just what Slocum was wondering."

Brenda came out of the kitchen with the coffeepot and refilled their cups. "Anything else I can get for you boys?" she asked.

"No, ma'am," said Stumpy. "This here coffee is just what I was craving."

"I'm satisfied, Brenda," said Speer.

"Just holler if you change your mind," she said, and she hustled off to tend to some other customers.

"Hey, Speer," said Stumpy. "Take a gander out the window."

Speer turned his head to look. He saw Slocum riding into town, leading a horse. A body was slung across the saddle of the extra horse. Speer raised his coffee cup and took a quick slug. "Ow," he said. "Goddamn. That's hot." He stood up and tossed his napkin down on the table. "Stay here and guard our place," he said. "I'll be right back." He hurried on out to the street and over to where Slocum was just dismounting. "Hey," he said. "Who you got there?"

"It's the one they call Rat's Ass," said Slocum. He lifted the head by the hair for Speer to get a look.

"Let's go down to the livery with the horses," said Speer. "I've got a cup of coffee getting cold."

They walked to the livery, where Speer told Dyer to take the body to the undertaker's and then put up the horses. Dyer grumbled about the extra duty, but Speer ignored him, and he and Slocum walked back to Brenda's Place. They went inside and sat down with Stumpy. Brenda brought Slocum some coffee. Then Stumpy saw what he had been watching for. Rowland and the other three men came walking out of the hotel.

"There they are," he said.

"Just keep watching them," said Slocum. "I have an idea that they're going to look for Rat's Ass."

"Tell us what happened," said Speer.

"I caught up with Rat's Ass," Slocum said. "He told me what I wanted to hear. Rowland and them killed the two cowboys and run off the cattle."

"Burned the barn?"

"Yeah. That too. He said he didn't know who it was that brought Rowland here, though."

"You believe him?"

"I think so. It don't matter, though, what I think about that."

"You ain't telling it all, Slocum," said the sheriff.

"Well, we kind of got into a tussle while I was quizzing him up. He got his gun, and I had to kill him."

"Where was you at?"

"Outside of your jurisdiction."

"At least that part's good. I'll just have to take your word for it."

"Them four is headed for the livery," said Stumpy.

Down the street, Dyer was leading Rats Ass, still slung across his saddle, to the undertaker's. Rowland saw him and raised a hand to signal his cohorts. "You boys just keep your mouths shut," he said. He hurried on over to intercept the liveryman with his putrid load. "Say, that's our pard you're lugging there."

Dyer stopped and looked at Rowland. "Yep," he said.

"How'd you get him?"

"Slocum and the sheriff brought him over here. This here horse and Slocum's horse had been rode, though. That's all I know."

Rowland turned and walked back to the other three. "Slocum killed him," he said. "I wonder did he talk first."

"What would he talk about?" said Cowley.

"About them two cowboys we kilt, of course," said Beebe.

"And the cattle and the barn," said Zeb Naylor.

Beebe suddenly looked worried. "Well," he said, "what do we do about it? Do we need to get the hell out of town?"

"No," said Rowland. "If he did talk to Slocum, it'll be Slocum's word against ours. Don't worry about it. Don't let anyone rattle your cages. That's all. Come on. Let's get back to the hotel."

"I'm hungry," said Cowley.

"Me too," said Zeb Naylor.

Rowland looked a little disgusted. He glanced at Beebe. Beebe nodded.

"All right," said Rowland. "All right. Let's go."

Back inside Brenda's Place, Stumpy said, "They're headed thisaway."

"My guess," said Slocum, "is that they were fixing to ride out after Rat's Ass. They saw his body and got no more reason to ride out."

"What should I do when they come in here?" said Speer. "Should I arrest them?"

"Not yet," Slocum said. "We know they done it, but we still got no proof. And we still don't know who it is they're working for. We might needle them a little bit."

The door opened and Rowland came in followed by the others. They headed for a table, but Rowland paused by the table where Slocum, Stumpy, and the sheriff were seated.

"Slocum," Rowland said, "I hear you shot our little partner."

"Dead as I could do it," said Slocum.

"You kill him just for meanness, or did you have some reason?"

"He pointed a gun at me," said Slocum.

"Well, I reckon that's reason enough. He always was a little bit anxious."

"He talked to me a little first," said Slocum.

"Oh, yeah? What about?"

"He told me that you boys killed those two cowhands out at Mix's place. Run off his cattle and burned his barn."

"He said that, did he?"

"He did."

"Wonder how come he'd say something like that?"

"He said you'd slapped him around some," Slocum said. "He was fed up with you and was cutting out on you."

"Oh, yeah. Well, that much was true. He was rude to the lady in here. I slapped him around a little for that. I guess he was pissed off about that. He must a been trying to get even with me for that when he told you that other stuff."

"I figured you'd say something like that," said Speer.

"It's the only thing I can think of," Rowland said.

"I can think of another reason," Speer said. "It's the truth."

"Think what you want to, Sheriff," Rowland said. "Thinking is one thing. Proving it's another."

"How come you walked to the livery and then come back?" said Slocum.

"What?"

"Was you riding out after Rat's Ass?"

"Oh. I get your meaning. Naw, we was just out for a morning walk, and then I seen that man toting what's left of Rat's Ass off. I walked over to see what had happened. That's all."

"We wouldn't ride out nowhere without our breakfast," said Beebe.

Rowland gave Beebe a look that told him to keep his mouth shut. "If you gents will excuse us," he said, "my boys here is awful hungry."

"You just watch your step," said Speer. " 'Cause we'll be watching your every move."

"Watch away, Sheriff. We got nothing to hide." He turned and walked over to another table, followed by his gang. They sat down and Brenda brought them coffee and took their orders. When she had gone back to the kitchen, Rowland and his gang talked in low tones.

Speer continued to give them a hard stare. "Goddamn it," he said, "I feel helpless as a damn baby. I'd sure like to slap them in jail."

"Be patient, Speer," Slocum said. "All we got to do is outlast them. They got to make a move sooner or later."

Slocum and his friends finished their coffee, paid out, and left. Stumpy kept looking over his shoulder as they walked away from Brenda's Place. When they got to the sheriff's office, he took a chair by the front window and continued watching. Speer took his seat behind the big desk.

"The sons of bitches," he said. "I'd like to—"

"Kill them?" said Slocum.

"Put them in jail," said Speer. "No. You're right. I'd like to kill them."

When Rowland and the other three finished their meals, Rowland stopped at the counter to pay. Brenda gave him change, and he said, "Ma'am, I hope you're not holding it against us what our former associate did in here."

"It's forgotten," she said.

"I sure do thank you for that," Rowland said. "He won't be bothering you no more. I can guarantee that. I just seen his body. I heard that Slocum killed him."

"Slocum killed him?" she said.

"That's what I heard. I got no idea what for." He tipped his hat. "Well, thank you again, ma'am. We'll be seeing you."

He led the way outside. The four men stood on the sidewalk for a moment.

"They're onto us, Rowland," said Beebe.

"Maybe we'd ought to cut out of here," Crowley said.

"We ain't going nowhere but to the hotel," Rowland said. "Come on."

* * *

"They're going back to the hotel," said Stumpy from his spot by the window.

"Just keep watching," said Slocum.

"It's all we can do," said Speer. "Goddamn it."

"They're on someone's payroll," said Slocum. "If they don't do something soon, he's going to get impatient. We can't get impatient first."

"I know you're right," said Speer. "It rankles me, though. They're working for whoever it is that's trying to get a war going between Mix and Ritchie? Is that what you're thinking?"

"That's my best idea," Slocum said. "If it ain't that, then it's either Mix or Ritchie out to get the other one."

"I think your first idea is the right one."

Out at the Mix spread, Mix was pacing the floor, fingering his six-gun. Helen had just brought out a coffeepot and two cups. She put them down on the table and stopped to stare at Mix. "Dave," she said, "will you stop that? Come over here and sit down. I got some fresh coffee."

Mix walked to the table and sat. Helen sat across from him. She poured them each a cup of coffee and shoved one across the table to him.

"You're making yourself crazy," she said.

"Someone killed two of our boys," he said.

"I know. They ran off our cattle and burned our barn. I know."

"Well, I feel like I got to do something about it."

"But what would you do? Kill James Ritchie? What if it's not him?"

"It's got to be Ritchie," Mix said. "There's no one else. Is there?"

"I don't know, Dave. I just don't know. Slocum thinks it's me. What about that?"

"I fired him."

"I know, but that's not the point. As sure as you are that it's Ritchie, Slocum could be that sure about me. We have to wait. We need some proof. Give it another week, Dave, before you do anything stupid."

Mix put his gun down on the table. "All right," he said. "But if we have any more trouble out here, all bets are off."

Back in Hangdog in their cramped hotel room, Rowland and the other three sat around in silence. Finally, Cowley stood up and paced the floor. Rowland stood it as long as he could. "Cut that out," he said. "Sit down."

"Hell," said Cowley, "I can't stand just setting around here like this."

"They're watching us," said Rowland.

"Well, what are we going to do?" said Beebe.

"Could we at least get a bottle of whiskey?" Zeb Naylor asked.

"We got to stay sober," Rowland said. "Play some cards."

"I ain't got enough cash to play cards," Cowley said. "This is making me crazy."

Rowland stood up. "All right," he said. "Goddamn it. I'll go see our employer. See if we can't scheme up some action. You three just sit tight here till I get back."

18

"We have to get rid of Slocum," said the female voice. The room in which they met was dark, and she was sitting in shadow. "And we have to be clever about it. There can be no mistakes."

"You have some idea?" Rowland said.

"He's sweet on Brenda," she said. "If you get Brenda, he'll come looking for her."

"But he and the other two are watching every move we make."

"You ride out of town," she said. "Slocum will follow you. While he's busy watching you, your three boys can snatch Brenda. There's an old line shack out on our ranch. I'll draw you a map. Have your boys take her there. After you've kept him out of town long enough, turn around and ride back. We'll have a note sent to Slocum. We'll tell him to come by himself if he wants to see her alive again. You can be waiting to ambush him along to the way."

"All right," Rowland said. "We'll do it. There's only one thing. Our cash is running low, and—"

She tossed him an envelope. He opened it and looked inside to see a stack of bills.

"There'll be more when the job's done," she said.

Rowland stood up and left the room.

Sitting by the window in the sheriff's office, Stumpy said, "Hey, Rowland's riding out."

Slocum hurried over to the window and looked out. "He's by himself," he said. "You stay here. I'll follow the son of a bitch."

"Be careful," Stumpy said.

"What if the others make a move?" said Speer.

"Watch them," said Slocum. He hurried out the door and hustled down the street to the livery to get his horse. Soon, he was on Rowland's trail.

Cowley and Zeb Naylor strolled out on the sidewalk. They rolled cigarettes and smoked, looking around nervously. Inside the sheriff's office, Stumpy watched them. "I think they're up to something," he said. "They just look kind of suspicious like."

Speer walked over to the window to join him in staring at the two culprits. "They ain't doing nothing," he said. "Where's the other one?"

"He must still be up in the room," Stumpy said.

But Beebe had gone out the back door of the hotel and walked the back way to the livery, where he got their horses and one extra. He had them all saddled, and he rode the long way around to Brenda's Place, where he left the horses behind her building. Then he walked the long way back, went back in the back door of the hotel, and walked out the front door.

"There he is," said Speer.

"Yeah," Stumpy said. "And there they go."

"They ain't going far on foot," said Speer.

"They're just going for a bite to eat," Stumpy said. "Looks like they're headed for Brenda's."

•   •   •

Out on the road, Slocum had gotten close enough to Rowland that he could keep his eye on him. He was careful, though, not to let Rowland see him. He was curious about where Rowland was going all alone. He recalled that Rowland's hired men apparently did not know who they were working for, and he thought that Rowland might be on his way to see his boss. He hoped so. It would be great to find out who it was. But he was not riding in the direction of the two ranches, Mix's or Ritchie's. If he was riding to meet his boss, it must be someone they had not thought of. Slocum was mighty curious.

It was almost closing time, and there were just a few customers in Brenda's Place when the three outlaws went in. They found a table and sat down. Brenda brought them coffee, and they ordered meals. She went back in the kitchen. One by one, the other customers finished their meals and paid. Soon, the three were the only ones left. Brenda brought their food. There were no witnesses around. Beebe stood up and pulled out his six-gun. He leveled it at Brenda.

"What is this?" she said. "A robbery?"

"We ain't going to steal nothing but you," Beebe said. "Head for the back door."

The other two stood up and stared hard at her. She thought for only an instant. She had no choice but to do as he said. She turned and walked through the kitchen, followed by the three hard cases. The went out the back door, where four saddled horses stood waiting. Cowley and Naylor mounted up. Beebe gestured toward the extra horse. "Climb on," he said. Brenda swung herself up into the saddle, and Beebe mounted his horse. He glanced at Cowley and Naylor. "You two ride behind her," he said. Then he looked at Brenda. "Follow me close." He started riding the long way around town toward the ranches.

• • •

Rowland stopped his horse and dismounted beside the road. Back on his trail, Slocum stopped. He found a spot where he could keep his eye on Rowland and he watched. The man sat down on a flat rock and took out a cigar. He lit it and puffed for a while. Then he got a bottle and a glass out of his saddlebags and poured himself a drink. He sat back down. Slocum thought that this must be his meeting place. Rowland was sitting casually smoking and having a drink. He must be waiting for someone.

Stumpy glanced at the clock on the sheriff's wall. "Speer," he said, "Them three ought to have come out of Brenda's by now."

Speer looked at the clock from behind his desk. "You're right," he said. "Let's go over there and see what's going on." He got up and grabbed his hat. Stumpy stood up and followed him out the door. They walked fast over to Brenda's. The door was unlocked, and they walked in, but they found the place empty. Speer walked into the kitchen. "Brenda," he called out, but he got no answer. He walked back into the main dining room. "She ain't here," he said. Stumpy was standing beside a table with three plates on it.

"Looky here," he said. "They ain't been touched."

Rowland stubbed out his cigar on the rock he had been sitting on, stood up and replaced the whiskey bottle and the glass in his saddlebags, and mounted his horse. Watching from his spot down the road, Slocum was puzzled. No one had showed up to meet with Rowland, and now Rowland was riding back toward town. Slocum pulled his horse into the brush beside the road and waited till Rowland rode past him. He waited a little longer. Then he mounted up to follow.

Rowland rode straight back into Hangdog, left his horse at the livery, and walked to the hotel. Wondering what the

hell was going on, Slocum rode to Speer's office. He found
Speer pacing the floor and Stumpy slumped in his chair beside the window.

"Slocum," said Speer, as Slocum stepped inside, "They
got Brenda."

"What? Who's got her?"

"Like you said, we watched them three," said Stumpy.
"We seen them go into Brenda's. We waited, and they
never come out again."

"So we walked over there and found the place open and
no one inside."

"There was three plates of food that no one had
touched," said Stumpy.

"Them three bastards had went in there and ordered
food," Speer said, "waited for everyone else to leave, and
then they must have snatched her and went out the back
door."

"Damn," said Slocum. "Did you look out back?"

"Sure," said Speer.

"Did you see any tracks?"

"None that was clear."

"Come on," Slocum said. "Let's go back over there."

He rode and the other two walked behind him as fast as
they could go. When they reached Brenda's Place, Slocum
was already out back checking the tracks.

"Can you tell anything?" Speer said.

"Not much more than what you already said. The
ground's pretty hard here. I'd say there was three, maybe
four horses, but I can't really tell which way they headed
when they left here."

"It's obvious that she was took away against her will,"
said Speer. "There's them three plates, and the door's unlocked."

"They got her all right," said Slocum. He ran outside
and mounted his horse.

"Where you going?" said Speer.

"After Rowland."

Slocum hurried over to the hotel, the other two following him on foot again, and he quickly dismounted and rushed inside. He ran up the stairs and down the hall to Rowland's room, where he reared back and kicked open the door. Pulling out his Colt, he rushed inside, but the room was empty. He looked around. Then he started back down the stairs. He met Speer and Stumpy about halfway down.

"He ain't there," he said. He did not slow down. He continued rushing down the stairs. Speer and Stumpy turned around to follow him again. Outside, Slocum was about to mount up again.

"Hold on," said Speer. "Where you going now?"

"I don't know," Slocum said, "but I got to find her."

"All right. All right," Speer said. "I want to find her too, but let's think this thing through. Why would anyone kidnap Brenda?"

"Why?" said Slocum.

"Yeah. Why?"

"I ain't the brains around here," said Stumpy, "but I say they done it to get to you."

"All right," Slocum said. "That makes sense."

"If they done it to get to you," Speer said, "they'll have to get in touch with you some way. Won't they?"

"Yeah," said Slocum. "I guess so."

"Then you don't want to go running off till they've got word to you," Stumpy said.

"I guess you're right," said Slocum. "But where the hell is Rowland?"

"Let's check at the livery," said Speer.

"He just dropped his horse off there," said Slocum. "I seen him do it."

"Come on," said Speer. "Let's check anyhow."

They walked down to the livery. Dyer was shoveling horse shit. He looked up when the three men came in. "You want horses?" he asked.

"No," said Speer. "Where's Rowland's horse?"

"He come and got it," said Dyer.

"He just dropped it off," said Slocum.

"Yeah," said Dyer. "He dropped it off and went away somewheres, and then he come back and got it again."

"Which way did he ride out?" said Speer.

"Damned if I know," Dyer said. "I got work to do. I can't be watching everyone who rides out of here."

Sitting in the line shack off the road, Brenda stared hard at her three captors. "All right," she said, "just what do you want with me?"

"We don't want a damn thing with you, missy," said Beebe. "What we want is Slocum."

"So that's it."

"That's it. That's all they is to it. So if you behave yourself, won't nothing happen to you."

"I can think of something we might want her for," said Cowley. He was looking longingly at Brenda.

"You better get your mind off a that," said Beebe. "Remember what happened to Rat's Ass? You take your rifle and go set outside and keep a watch. Maybe that'll get your mind off a what you're thinking about."

Cowley stood up and stomped out of the shack, slamming the door behind himself. Brenda still stared at Beebe.

"You mean, Slocum's going to come looking for me, and you're going to kill him?"

"That's the idea," said Beebe.

"And then you're just going to let me go?"

"Why, sure."

"If you think I'm stupid enough to believe that, then you've got another think coming."

"Why, how come we wouldn't let you go? We got nothing against you."

"I'll be a witness," she said.

"Naw," said Beebe. "We won't shoot him right here in front of you."

"I can charge you with kidnaping," she said.

"Now, why would you want to do that if we ain't going to hurt you? If you cooperate with us, you'll be all right."

"I know what to expect from you," she said. "I'm no fool."

Zeb Naylor was at the window. "Rowland's coming," he said. In another minute, Rowland opened the door and stepped inside. Cowley was still watching from in front of the shack. When Rowland stepped in, Brenda gave him a hard look. "I knew you were behind this," she said.

"You just keep quiet," Rowland said, "and I won't stuff a rag in your mouth. Zeb, tie her to that chair."

"Sure thing," said Zeb Naylor. He found a piece of rope and moved behind Brenda. She struggled as he tried to pull her wrists together behind her back. "Now, don't give me no trouble, lady," he said. Rowland stepped up quickly and slapped Brenda hard across the face.

"Set still," he said. "I could go on ahead and just kill you right now."

"Go ahead," she said. "That's what you mean to do anyway."

"We might need you alive," Rowland said. "And who knows, if you mind your manners, you might just live through this."

Brenda sat still while Naylor pulled her wrists behind the back of the chair and tied them tight. Beebe looked at Rowland.

"What do we do now?" he said.

"You're going to stay right in here with the gal," said Rowland. "If anyone besides us comes through that door, hold your six-gun right at her head. But I don't think they will. The rest of us is going to set up an ambush a little ways down the road. We'll get him before he gets here."

• • •

"How the hell did Rowland get out of town?" Slocum said. He was stomping around the floor in Speer's office. Speer, who was every bit as anxious as was Slocum, could hardly stand it.

"Why the hell don't you set down?" said the sheriff. "You're making me crazy." Slocum sat in a chair against the wall. "That part's easy," the sheriff continued. "They played us for suckers. Rowland led you out of town while the others grabbed Brenda. Then he led you back to town. When we told you what had happened, and the three of us went tearing over to Brenda's, Rowland got his horse back and lit out."

"I'm going to kill that son of a bitch," Slocum said.

"Yeah," said Speer, "but not too soon. We got to get Brenda back in one piece."

"I know that," Slocum said. "I won't kill him right off. I might stomp him up some."

"If we knowed who it was paying Rowland," said Stumpy, "we might could figure out where to look."

"Yeah," said Slocum, "but we don't know."

Just then the door opened and Ryan Walter, the clerk from the hotel, walked in. He looked at the sheriff and at Stumpy, and then walked straight over to Slocum. He held out an envelope toward Slocum.

"Someone left this at the hotel for you," he said.

Slocum grabbed it and tore it open.

"Who left it?" said Speer.

"I don't know," said Walter. "I was away from the desk for just a minute. When I come back, it was laying on the counter. I never seen who left it."

"All right," said Speer. "You can go on back to work now." Walter hesitated. "Go on," said Speer. "Get out a here."

Walter hustled his ass on out of the office. Speer and Stumpy both looked at Slocum. Slocum read out loud.

"It says, 'Slocum, if you want to see the woman alive

again, follow the enclosed map to the old line shack on the Ritchie ranch. Come alone.' "

"Let me see the map," said Speer. He grabbed it from Slocum's hand and studied it. "I know where this is. It's out of the way. Ain't been used for a spell. Let's get going."

"Hold on," said Slocum. "You heard what the note said. I'm going alone."

19

Slocum rode hard and fast. He followed the map that some unknown person had left for him. He did not ride the main road out to the ranch. He had to ride around to the far back side of Ritchie's place and then take a small trail that looked almost unused. He could tell that a few horses had been over it very recently, but he figured that it had been abandoned before that for some time. This part of the ranch was heavily treed. He was riding through a thickly wooded corner of the ranch. As he rode, he thought about the location, the Ritchie ranch. He wondered if it had been Ritchie all along. He couldn't be sure, but it was certainly beginning to look suspicious. Going through the wooded area, he forced himself to stop thinking along those lines. He knew that Rowland and his bunch were laying for him out here somewhere. He had to stay alert. As the terrain shifted to rolling hills, still tree-covered, he slowed his horse. He started looking around in all directions as he moved along the narrow trail.

Unknown to Slocum, Speer and Stumpy were riding along behind him. They stayed well back, for Slocum had insisted on riding out alone. They had let him go, but then they had followed. They knew the same thing that Slocum knew. He was supposed to come out alone. They knew also that it was a trap, planned to get Slocum. The showdown was near, and they knew that as well. They had no intention of allowing Slocum to be caught in an ambush with no backup. They did not ride as hard or as fast as Slocum did, for they did not want him to know they were behind him.

"What're we going to do, Sheriff?" Stumpy asked as they moved down the trail between the trees.

"We'll just play it by ear," said Speer. "We don't know what's going to happen. I imagine, though, that those bastards will lay an ambush for Slocum somewhere along this trail."

"I'll bet you what," said Stumpy.

"What's that?"

"I'll bet you're right."

In her apartment in Hangdog, Margaret Ritchie changed into her riding clothes and strapped on a six-gun. She was about to go out the door when James Ritchie walked into the room.

"Margaret," he said. "Where are you going?"

"I'm just going out for a ride," she said.

"I don't think you should be going out alone," Ritchie said.

"Oh, don't worry, dear," she said. "I'll be all right."

"I should go with you," he said.

"James," she said, "I need to be alone to think, to relax. Don't worry about me. I'll be just fine."

"How long will you be gone?"

"Give me a couple of hours," she said.

"If you're not back by then—"

"Then you come riding to my rescue. All right?"

"All right. Where will you ride?"

"I think I'll ride north. There hasn't been any trouble out that way. It will be perfectly safe."

"Stay on the road," Ritchie said. "If I don't see you back here in two hours, I'm coming after you."

She left the hotel, went down to the livery for a horse, and rode south out of town.

Brenda struggled with her ropes, but they were much too tight, and she was not making any headway. She wasn't sure what she would do, even if she could get them off, but she felt like she needed to help Slocum somehow. These rats had used her to lay a trap for him. She had to do something. Beebe was not paying any attention to her. Anticipating the ambush, he was standing at the open front door of the shack and staring out down the trail. Finally, near desperation, Brenda realized that her hands were not tied to the chair. They were only tied together behind the chair back. She stood up slowly and carefully. Her hands were still tied, but she was free from the chair. She walked slowly so as not to make any noise, and she came up behind Beebe. She stood for a moment gathering all of her courage. She looked at his ass. His legs were slightly spread. She knew she could do it. She took careful aim, and she kicked with all her strength.

Her foot came up between his legs and around under his crotch, catching him with a firm, hard slap against his balls. He screamed in pain and surprise, and he doubled over, clutching at his injured jewels with both hands. Brenda raised her foot again, put it on his ass and shoved with all her might. Beebe sprawled on the ground out in front of the shack. Brenda hurried out and kicked him in the head. She wished that she had been wearing her boots, but she kicked as hard as she could, using the heel of her shoe.

"Aagh," Beebe groaned.

Brenda kicked again. This time she caught him full in the face and smashed his nose.

"Aah, I'm blind," Beebe roared.

She hoped that he wasn't lying. She squatted beside him, her back to him, and watching him, reached down with her still-tied hands to pull the six-gun out of his holster. Then she quickly stood up again. Remembering that he had a rifle in the shack, she went back inside and found it. Backing up to it, she gripped it in her other hand. Then she ran out of the shack and headed for the trees. Beebe was still rolling on the ground and groaning. His face was a mass of blood-covered, raw flesh.

Out on the trail, Slocum came to a place with a sharp left turn. He stopped and considered the possibilities. He thought that he was getting close to the shack. He did not know what was around the corner. He dismounted and tied his horse to a small tree just beside the trail. Then he moved into the trees and continued on his way. He got around the curve like that, and he looked ahead. The hills rose up along the left side of the road. It would be a good spot for an ambush. He did not really want to get into a gunfight with Rowland and his gang. Likely, they had left someone in the shack with Brenda, and if he thought that Slocum had a fighting chance, he might kill her. He moved cautiously forward. His eyes caught a glint ahead up on the side of the hill, the same side of the trail that he was on. He eased himself ahead.

Margaret rode up to the Mix ranch house and dismounted. Helen stepped out on the porch. "Margaret," she said. "What brings you out this way? I haven't seen you out riding since the days when we used to ride together."

"I have to see your husband," Margaret said.

"Well, sure. I'll just get him. He's in the house. Well, come on in."

"I haven't much time," Margaret said.

She followed Helen into the house, where Helen called out Mix's name. He came out of the bedroom. "What is it?" he was saying, and then he saw Margaret. "Oh. Hello."

"Dave," said Margaret, "I just found out that Rowland and his men have kidnaped Brenda. They left Slocum a note telling him to ride out alone to a line shack on our ranch if he wanted see her alive again."

"They'll kill him," said Mix.

"That's likely," Margaret said. "I couldn't find the sheriff, so I came to see you."

"Tell me where the shack is," said Mix. "I'll ride out there right now."

"Dave," said Helen.

"He's my friend," said Mix. "I can't let him ride into a trap like that."

"There's not time for me to give you directions," Margaret said. "Come on. I'll show you."

"Let me change," said Helen. "I'll go with you."

"There's not time," Margaret said.

Mix finished strapping on his six-gun, and he followed Helen outside. "I'll just have to get a horse saddled," he said.

In town James Ritchie, nervous about his wife's ride, walked to the livery for a horse. He found Dyer brushing one of his tenants. "What can I do for you, Mr. Ritchie?" said Dyer.

"I need a horse," said Ritchie. "I let Margaret ride out of here alone, and I shouldn't have done that, even if she was riding north. I should have gone with her."

"I'll get you a horse in a jiffy," Dyer said, "but she didn't ride north."

"What?"

"I seen her head out of town going south," Dyer said.

Ritchie got the horse and headed south, but he stopped by the sheriff's office. He went inside, but no one was there. He was about to leave again when he noticed a note lying on the floor. He picked it up. It was in Margaret's handwriting. He stuffed it in his pocket and hurried back out to his horse. Mounting up, he rode fast. The note had said that there was a map with it, but he had not seen the map. It referred to a line shack on the Ritchie ranch, though. He knew where that was.

Slocum had crept through the woods until he was close enough to the glint to see that it was indeed a man holding a rifle. He could see that it was the one known as Zeb Naylor. He could not get any closer without making too much noise, and he still did not want to get into a gunfight. He did not know where the others were hidden or how many of them were out there. He could easily have shot Naylor dead, but he couldn't risk the shot. Looking around, he spotted a rock on the ground that looked to be about the size of a baseball. He picked it up and hefted it. He looked back at Naylor. He was looking at the side of his head. Naylor took off his hat and wiped his forehead with a sleeve. Slocum drew back his arm and threw a mighty swing. The rock whistled its way through the air and smacked Naylor hard on the side of the head. Naylor dropped over at once. Slocum hurried down to Naylor and inspected his handiwork. Naylor was out cold all right. Slocum took his handgun and his rifle. He started looking around for the others.

Safe in the woods, Brenda thought about what to do. Rowland and the other two must be somewhere between her and Slocum, and if she tried to reach Slocum, they would surely spot her and catch her. She couldn't afford that, but she had to warn Slocum of the ambush. She decided that she would start the shooting. Careful to point the barrel away from her, she twisted her wrist and cocked the hammer of the six-gun. Then she pulled the trigger. The report was incredibly loud there in the quiet woods. She cocked the hammer again and pulled the trigger again, and again, and again, and again.

• • •

Rowland heard the shots. They came from back toward the shack. Something had gone wrong. No one had fired at Slocum yet. He knew that. There was no one in the shack but Beebe and the woman. It didn't make sense. He had to investigate. He stood up and looked around, and he could see Cowley hunkered down behind a rock. He could not see Naylor.

"Cowley," he called out.

"Yeah."

"I got to go to the shack and check on them shots. You and Naylor stay here and get Slocum when he comes along."

"We'll get him," said Cowley.

Back down the trail, Speer and Stumpy heard the shots. "It's started," Speer said. "Let's go." He kicked his horse in the sides and it leaped ahead. Stumpy did the same.

A little farther back, Margaret and Mix heard the shots as well. They looked at one another. "We may be too late," Margaret said.

"Let's get up there," said Mix.

Slocum was moving through the woods on the side of the hill. He knew that someone was shooting, but he had no idea who it was. All it meant to Slocum was that there was no longer any need for silence on his part. He went up higher on the hillside, and at last he spotted Cowley down below. He saw no reason to give any of these dirty bastards any warning. He raised his Colt and took aim, and just then, the rocky ground under his feet seemed to give way. He slipped and went tumbling. The noise alerted Cowley, who turned quickly. It took him a minute to locate the source of the noise. When he spotted Slocum, Slocum was scrambling back to his feet. Cowley raised his rifle to his shoulder and fired. Slocum threw himself to one side and went rolling again. The shot had missed him. Cowley cranked another round into the chamber and raised the rifle again, but Slocum was back on his feet, Colt in hand. Slocum fired. The bullet smacked Cowley in the chest sending him falling backward down the hillside. He was stopped by a tree trunk. He lay still. Slocum figured he was dead. At any rate, he was surely incapacitated, and Slocum did not feel like he had any time to waste on the son of a bitch. He hurried on.

Brenda could not handle the rifle with her hands tied behind her back, and the six-gun was empty. She dropped both of them in a bush. She did not know what to do now. She only hoped that she had warned Slocum in time. Something made her turn around and look back toward the shack. She saw that Beebe was sitting up and holding his head. She decided to move a little farther into the woods. Then she saw Rowland. Luckily, he did not see her. He came out of the woods a little farther down, and he ran toward the shack. Fascinated, she watched.

Rowland made it to the shack. He stepped up to the wretched Beebe. He looked inside. The place was empty. Turning on Beebe, he said, "Where's the girl?"

"She broke my nose," Beebe whined.

"Where is she?"

"I don't know. I can't even see."

"You stupid shit," said Rowland. He had heard shots all around, and he figured that things were falling apart. He raised his six-gun and fired into Beebe's head. Then he rushed around behind the shack to find his horse. He mounted up and rode out fast in the opposite direction from all the action.

•   •   •

Brenda turned around to head deeper into the woods, and she ran right into Slocum. Startled, she let out a little cry.

"It's okay, Brenda," Slocum said. "It's just me."

"Oh, God," she said, "I was afraid they might've killed you."

"I was worried about you," he said. "Here. Let me get those ropes off of you."

He untied her and rubbed her hands and wrists. Things were quiet again.

"I got two of them," Slocum said, "but there's still two more."

"No," she said. "One of them's over there in front of the shack. Rowland killed him. Then he rode out that way."

She nodded in the direction Rowland had run.

"I've got to catch him," said Slocum. "I've got to find out who hired him. My horse is back this way." He indicated the direction down the trail from which he had come.

"There's horses behind the shack," Brenda said.

They walked toward the shack, just as Speer and Stumpy came riding down the trail. Each man had a gun in his hand.

"You can put them away, boys," Slocum said. "It's all over here." He filled them in on the details as he continued on his way to the horses.

Margaret figured she was close enough to the action. She wanted Mix to be found at the site of the shootings. She did not know if Rowland and the others had gotten Slocum or not. Either way, if Mix was found dead nearby, he would be implicated. She slowed her horse just enough to allow Mix to get ahead. Then she pulled out her six-gun. "Dave," she yelled. "Slow down. There's something over here." She stopped her horse. Mix stopped his, turned, and rode back to her. She leveled the gun at him.

"What's this, Margaret?" he said. "You?"

"It's been me all along, Dave," she said. "Now this is the end of the road for you."

"Margaret, why?"

"It's all for James," she said. "He was always too wishy-washy. We're going to own this whole valley."

She cocked the revolver. Just then her husband came riding up behind her. "Margaret," he shouted. "What are you doing?"

"Dave's been behind all this," she said. "I'm going to kill him."

"Don't, Margaret."

From the other direction, Slocum, Brenda, Speer, and Stumpy came riding.

"What's going on here?" shouted Speer.

"I've got to kill Dave," said Margaret. "It's been him all along."

Ritchie jerked out his revolver and fired. His bullet hit Margaret between the shoulder blades. She jerked. She tried to fire, but her hand went limp. She slid sideways off her horse and fell to the ground. Ritchie rushed to her side. He jumped off his horse and knelt beside her. She was not dead.

"Margaret," he said. By then, Speer was standing right behind him. Slocum and the others had ridden up close. "Why?" said Ritchie. "Why?"

"It was all for you, James," she said. "I had to do it. You were just too soft." Then her eyes closed and her breathing stopped. She was dead.

20

The girl would identify him, Rowland knew. He did not know if his last two men had killed Slocum or not. Slocum might have killed them for all he knew. He only knew that he had to get the hell out of the territory, but he needed more cash to go on. He meant to slip back into town without being seen, look in on Mrs. Ritchie, and demand more money. If she refused him, he would threaten to expose her. He had to have the money. The day was coming to an end, and darkness would aid him in sneaking around. He would be very careful.

Slocum had tried to track Rowland, but he'd had no luck. He rode back to town with the others. They all went into Brenda's Place, where Brenda got rid of the leftover, untouched meals and fixed them all some fresh food and poured coffee all around. They all sat down together. "It don't seem right letting you do all this for us after what you been through," said Speer.

"It's all right," Brenda said. "I need something to do."

"It was real brave, what you done out there," Stumpy said.

"I had to do something."

Ritchie was not with them. He had told Mix that he would sell out to him and leave the country. Mix had argued with him, but Ritchie had insisted. He couldn't hang around after what Margaret had done. He had to go somewhere else and start over. It was the only way. They had checked Cowley and Zeb Naylor and found them both dead. It was all over except for Rowland, and Slocum planned to go after him at daylight. Mix had apologized to Slocum.

"That's all right," Slocum had said. "A man has to defend his wife. And besides, you come after me when the chips was down. I won't forget that."

When they had finished eating, Mix excused himself to get back to the ranch. Speer also decided to leave. Stumpy said, "I got to get me some shut-eye too. It's been a long day."

When they had all left, Brenda looked at Slocum. "Will you stay with me tonight?" she asked.

They lay side by side in Brenda's bed naked. Slocum knew that she needed gentle love. He entered her slow and easy. He kissed her and fondled her breasts while he slowly moved in and out.

"You're wonderful," he said.

"Oh, Slocum," she said. She held him tightly as he continued to move in her body.

Rowland arrived in Hangdog in the wee hours of the morning. He had taken the long way around to avoid being seen. He rode in behind the buildings, and he slipped in the back door of the hotel. He made his way to the Ritchies' apartment and tried the door. It was locked. He had to have that money. He shoved the door. It did not budge. He bashed his shoulder against it. Inside, Ritchie heard the noise. He got up, picked up his six-gun, and went to the door.

"Who's there?" he said.

"It's me. Rowland. I got to see your wife."

Ritchie thought for a moment. Rowland had run away from the scene of the conflict early. He did not know the outcome. He must think that Margaret was still alive. Margaret had hired Rowland. Ritchie knew that now. He did not hate Margaret, but he hated Rowland. It was illogical, but he still hated the son of a bitch.

"Just a minute," he said. "I'll get her."

He walked away from the door and cocked his six-gun. Then he walked back and opened the door. Rowland found himself staring into the barrel of a gun.

"Wait," he said. "Don't—"

But Ritchie pulled the trigger, shattering the silence of the night, and splattering Rowland's brains against the wall on the other side of the hallway.

Watch for

SLOCUM AND THE TONTO BASIN WAR

335th novel in the exciting SLOCUM series
from Jove

Coming in January!

Don't miss a year of

Slocum Giant
by
Jake Logan

Slocum Giant 2004:
Slocum in the Secret Service
0-515-13811-8

Slocum Giant 2005:
Slocum and the Larcenous Lady
0-515-14009-0

B900

JAKE LOGAN
TODAY'S HOTTEST ACTION WESTERN!

J. R. ROBERTS

THE GUNSMITH

Explore the exciting Old West with one of the men who made it wild!

Penguin Group (USA) Online

What will you be reading tomorrow?

Tom Clancy, Patricia Cornwell, W.E.B. Griffin,
Nora Roberts, William Gibson, Robin Cook,
Brian Jacques, Catherine Coulter, Stephen King,
Dean Koontz, Ken Follett, Clive Cussler,
Eric Jerome Dickey, John Sandford,
Terry McMillan, Sue Monk Kidd, Amy Tan,
John Berendt...

You'll find them all at
penguin.com

*Read excerpts and newsletters,
find tour schedules and reading group guides,
and enter contests.*

Subscribe to Penguin Group (USA) newsletters
and get an exclusive inside look
at exciting new titles and the authors you love
long before everyone else does.

PENGUIN GROUP (USA)
us.penguingroup.com